The Death Mask

The Death Mask

The Mapleview Series – Book 1

Tom Raimbault

Published 2015 by Creativia

Book design by Creativia (www.creativia.org)

Cover art by http://www.thecovercollection.com/

This book is a work of fiction. Names, characters, places, and incidents are the product of the author's imagination or are used fictitiously. Any resemblance to actual events, locales, or persons, living or dead, is purely coincidental.

Preface

I've sometimes mentioned of having near lifelike encounters with the characters in Mapleview—Amber, Mary, Ekaterina and the likes. (Don't worry; you'll learn about these other characters in later books of the Mapleview series.) Much of this phenomenon of physically encountering them can surely be attributed to my overactive writer's imagination. The phenomenon began by taking notice of women who reminded me of Amber, Mary, Ekaterina and the likes—at least how they would appear in my mind while writing of them. Perhaps it's natural for the mind to place in reality someone who is sorely missed. And perhaps without realizing it, I triggered a self-induced spell of phantasming while writing of Amber.

It might sound like a cool thing. But you see, Amber is terribly aggressive as an author's phantom. You see; in contrast to the other characters of Mapleview, it isn't enough for her to simply appear in the face of some other woman. She deliberately goes out of her way to interact with me. She'll smile or wave; sometimes nearly get in my face with a friendly greeting. And it didn't take long for me to realize that the physical women involved in this phenomenon were unaware of it.

Amber, by far, created for me the most hauntings while writing of her. She has the power to briefly weave herself in another person for purposes of carrying out her simple will. In short, I have succeeded in inadvertently conjuring up a "familiar spirit" and then watching it possess other people. And if that weren't enough, the thing calls out to me through some telepathic means. I've sometimes been awakened at night from the assumed calling of Amber, wondering where I am at. Throughout the day I fight her invasion of my mental privacy. Amber is persistent. There's a heavy feeling of sadness as she begs me not to abandon her and just give her a chance. She's not as bad as I might believe. Amber urges that she is a really nice person.

Needless to say this is frightening for me. Have I lost my mind? Has writing caused me difficulty in differentiating fiction from reality?

Then came the day when I formulated a solution. Amber needed to be given her own, special place in the forest where I could visit her on a regular basis. Perhaps this would put a stop to weaving herself in nearby people or mentally calling out to me in the middle of the night, asking where I am.

So I found Amber a special, little landscape in the forest and dedicated it to her. A couple times a week I would visit and perform my secret calling. In addition, I would bring pieces of chocolate and leave it in the area so that Amber would feel all-the-more special.

Guess what? Amber was not satisfied with her landscape! Somehow she guided me to a place at the opposite end of the forest and urged me to dedicate that place as our special place.

"Oh, Amber; it's beautiful! I can see why you prefer this area." I exclaimed

I now visit her in this place and continue to offer my special calling along with gifts of chocolate. In recent days I have brought with wine and decorated the ground with it to intoxicate her spirit and hopefully ease her inhibitions. One morning in the not-so-distant future, I will bring with a red rose; and kiss the petals that are surely as delicate as her sweet lips. The rose will be left in the forest along with the usual gifts of chocolate and wine. Perhaps these simple gestures of kindness will charm and invoke the imaginary spirit of Amber to oversee the success of this Mapleview series, maybe even ensure that it is all-the-more enjoyable for you.

Tom Raimbault

Frankfort, Illinois

September 5, 2011

Chapter One

Distanced by 10.6 miles of a rural highway named Route 4, Sillmac has long been a neighboring community of the charming town of Mapleview. Mapleview was established in the 1830s, but it wasn't until 1872, precisely, that the town of Sillmac established itself. As originally described in The Tree Goddess, Sillmac is similar to Mapleview as it has its share of restaurants, shops and even small museums for the town's yearly tourists. But Sillmac is considered a prestigious area in comparison to Mapleview. Taxes are higher, housing with no set price. Whatever you ask for your home; it will definitely sell as no one can set a price on Sillmac.

The historical residences and places of business have been renovated to eliminate any appearance of decay and maintain that 1870s charm. And just like Mapleview, the town is surrounded by thick, forested wilderness. Many of the preserves have been improved to the point of qualifying as botanical gardens with paved, nature trails outlined in beautiful flowers; countless ponds with lily pads and meditational gardens at the center of flowing creeks.

Make no mistake about it; Sillmac is a town where the elite few reside. And it isn't uncommon for those with happy stories of success and extreme wealth to live in Sillmac. Take for example married couple, Michael and Linsey, and their daughter, Paulette. Michael was founder of the now nationwide chain of hardware stores called Dickly's Hardware. Merely opening his first hardware store in downtown Mapleview, Dickly's hardware soon grew at an exponential rate which rewarded Michael the ability to purchase and own an enormous region of wilderness at the outskirt of Sillmac. In that region of wilderness; he had an enormous, castle-like mansion built for him, his wife and daughter to live in. The very center of the estate is what could be described as a miniature, forested mountain with that castle-like mansion sitting buried under thick trees.

But despite their great fortune, Michael and Linsey would soon see much misfortune on a morning in 1987 when their nine-year-old daughter, Paulette, had a terrible accident that would change her and the family's life forever. Keep in mind that the family lived at the top of a miniature mountain. Paulette had the wild inclination that morning to coast on her bike down one of the sides.

On that morning, she ignored her instincts, feeling that overcoming her fears and venturing down the slope would have made her all the braver along with providing some much needed excitement. With only a gentle push over the edge, an overwhelming force of gravity pulled her faster and faster down the slope. There was no turning back for Paulette as the velocity rapidly increased. She maintained firm hold on the handlebars and stayed in control for a few seconds. But the child didn't anticipate that the landscape would soon turn treacherous not more than halfway down the forested slope. A rocky formation with large, moss-colored boulders soon suggested a terrible danger. Naturally, she applied her coaster brake to avoid surfaces that could never be biked on—at least at a high speed.

Despite its reputation for a mild disposition, a timber rattlesnake was startled at the sound of Paulette's back tire that scraped along the soil, kicking up dust while rapidly approaching. The snake had no choice but to strike at whatever danger approached. Its fangs pierced the bicycle's front tires. Paulette had seen the snake's attack and screamed just as the tire popped. She toppled over the handlebars and continued her high-speed descent in the form of somersaults. The only thing on her mind at that moment was whether or not the ugly snake was near. Of course the sensation of branches, occasional leaves and anything else touching her on the ground were believed to be the snake coming to get her. The young girl screamed while desperately trying to get away. This only added to her rapid descent of somersaults.

In reality, the snake lay injured near the bike and was the least of Paulette's worries. She continued to somersault herself out of control until spiraling over a small drop which landed in a region of boulders. This final smash that was fueled by such incredible momentum not only broke her neck and damaged an area of her spinal cord, but caused injury to the posterior inferior frontal gyrus of her brain—more commonly referred to as Broca's region (responsible for speech and language comprehension).

Young Paulette was a mangled up mess, unconscious and bleeding from the head. And how was she rescued in such an isolated area? Mothers have a keen sense of intuition. Linsey received an unusual surge of anxiety at the moment her daughter pushed off the hill. Within a minute her face flushed with a God-awful terror. She knew beyond the shadow of a doubt that Paulette was in trouble.

"Paulette? Paulette!" The frantic woman ran along the outside of the castle-like mansion, desperately searching for her daughter. Had someone hiked up the miniature mountain to hide on the forested property with the purpose of abducting the young girl? Ironically, the easiest and most logical slope to hike down while wondering this was the one Paulette descended.

Linsey nervously cried and wiped her tears while hiking down the slope, all the while just knowing that her daughter was in grave danger. Was she descending the right slope? Should she have turned around and looked elsewhere? But some distance down the slope could be seen Paulette's bicycle lying on the ground. Linsey quickly jogged downwards while calling out to her daughter. Finally reaching the bicycle, Linsey took notice of the injured snake that looked to have been run over by a tire. Maybe Paulette was bitten and now lay unconscious.

But no, it was far worse than that! Imagine the shock of seeing your child laying face-first on a treacherous terrain of boulders with a small pool of blood running near her head. Would you grab your cell phone and call for the paramedics? This wouldn't have been possible in 1987, even for the wealthy. There were no cell phones in people's pockets in those days, especially in a deeply rural area. And although Linsey wished to run to her daughter, some part of her knew that every second counted! It was an adrenaline-fueled flight back up the slope that nearly caused a young woman a heart attack.

Broca's region is interesting. Although we label the area responsible for generating speech and understanding language, it really isn't. People who have sustained injuries and damage to this part of the brain have been able to resume speech some months later. It seems that other areas of the brain are capable of taking over whatever responsibility the Broca region has. And you would think that for such a young girl, Paulette would have restored this vital function of generating words. But nothing intelligible could be produced. With only grunts that soon turned to frustration, it was easier to maintain communication with the girl by playing charades and verifying a "yes" or "no" with one blink of the eyes or two, soon to be replaced with nods by the time she hopefully restored use of her neck.

As hoped, Paulette's broken neck healed and regained the ability to move through therapy. But spinal cord damage from some apparent, blunt trauma during the descent had left Paulette unable to move from the neck, down.

Fortunately, Michael and Linsey's wealth allowed at home therapy and some schooling from the finest teachers who specialized in disabled children. But no matter how much therapy was provided for forming sound into talking, Paulette was unable to create intelligible words.

* * *

This tragedy took place only several miles from where Amber lived and grew up. On that morning, Amber would have been a teenage girl of fifteen years old. In Sillmac, many of the homes are independently seated on acres and acres of untamed wilderness, just like Michael and Linsey's home. But Amber's parents lived in the beautifully wooded subdivision of Settler's View that shared a street with other enormous homes that averaged a modest price of $950,000 to just over $1,000,000. This, of course, is being compared with much larger homes (like Michael and Linsey's) that sat on thirty acres or more of wilderness that would go for... well; let's just say much, much more!

You and I can only dream of owning a home in the Settler's View subdivision. And people who live this sort of lifestyle must be very different from you and me. But don't think for one second that Amber grew up to be a spoiled, little brat. Mother made sure that her daughter was a down-to-Earth lady who would have an understanding of those intangible things that are most important in life, while at the same time having an appreciation for what is simple and true. There was, however, one small, negative quality of Amber. The girl had a relentless drive with a Hell-bent intent to get exactly what she wanted. But don't we all possess that quality of desiring what we want to some degree?

The word amber draws to mind a few things. One might think of a woman's name or the fossilized tree resin that makes the precious stone found in jewelry, or perhaps simply a radiant fire. Amber is an interesting color. You cannot precisely identify one color as officially being amber as it includes various shades of orange. And when we say that a woman has amber-colored hair, it could be anywhere from a dark blonde, to a light brown, or possibly a light red.

With a name like Amber, one would expect her to have been born with amber-colored hair. But she wasn't. Amber was born with strands of brown that grew into the most beautiful, long, flowing, light-brown hair that often changed shades throughout the years. Then again, I suppose at times that people might have considered her hair to be amber-colored, being that the color varies throughout different shades.

So just how did Amber get her name? While still in the womb; Amber would often accompany Mother for leisurely strolls through one of the forested paths in Sillmac where Mother had the lovely practice of talking to her soon-to-be newborn. She would stop to rest near an open creek and rub her abdomen while speaking out loud to the baby. This, she believed, would allow the unborn child to bond with her and maybe realize that there was a world outside. And maybe the child understood Mother. But Mother had so many questions—as many new mothers do during pregnancy. She knew the baby would be born a girl. But what would the baby look like? Who would she grow up to be?

One morning, Mother brought with a plastic bowl on the hike, and bent down to her special creek to fill it with water. The bowl was brought home, and the water saved for later that night.

While her husband slept in the late evening hours, she filled the water from the creek into a clear, quartz bowl; then brought it out to the backyard deck where it was set on the table with a candle behind.

An ordinary glass bowl filled with tap water would have been so unflattering in a moment of scrying. Aside from that, she wanted the water from her special creek where she and the baby shared a moment each day. Scrying, in case you are unaware, involves gazing into a crystal ball, or into water, with the purpose of seeking visions. Many find the greatest effect by gazing through the water at a candle flame, or observing the flame through the reflection in the water. It is the objective to put one's self in a trance while maintaining a fixed gaze.

Gazing at the candle through a quartz bowl that was filled with creek water would have certainly had the greatest effect for visions of her soon-to-be-newborn child. It was truly a powerful moment of scrying. But the only vision seen was the most beautiful, brilliant color of amber. At that moment, Mother decided that her daughter would be named Amber.

So many hopes for her daughter in that powerful moment: Amber would be a most-beautiful woman throughout her life. Perhaps her heart would be great, loving all those around her with a nurturing air, and yet a sense of untamed freedom that would enable her to pursue her dreams, even bring a certain magic into her own family as she would be the very source that kept the home alive. These were the hopes that Mother had for her baby while little Amber resided in the womb.

As a girl, it certainly appeared that Amber was growing up to be all that Mother hoped for. But despite her imposed modesty and earthly beauty, Amber had an unusual gift that was learned at an early age. Amber had the power to get anything desired. It wasn't like a young girl who begs mommy and daddy for that new toy, soon to be those expensive jeans or that new car. The world is full of these high-maintenance, bratty women who have learned to get what they want through badgering and rude behavior. No, Amber remained well-mannered in the face of Mother and Father while keeping knowledge of this unusual gift to herself. She found a true power behind fantasy in which she would harness and channel every emotion she could find and direct it towards her desire until it finally materialized in reality.

She learned just how powerful this gift was on a summer day at the age of eleven when thoroughly fed up with a girl her age who lived next door. Michelle was terribly envious of Amber and hated her to the very core. Being that she despised Amber, she often made critical remarks of just about anything Amber did and said. Amber would laugh and have fun with her friends and then suddenly close off and shut down once Michelle entered the picture. Nothing out of the ordinary could be done and said when in the presence of Michelle. And even while Amber remained still and quiet, Michelle found it appropriate to call out Amber's sudden disconnect.

On that summer day, Michelle's mother had taken the young girl to the beauty salon for a makeover and hair styling. Now these were merely girls who would enter sixth grade in September. And keep in mind that although it's a common practice in modern times for those with extra money to take a child to a beauty spa for a makeover, it was a rare occurrence in 1983. But being that this was the prestigious town of Sillmac, it was appropriate for eleven-year-old Michelle to be treated to a makeover before a family barbeque that was to be held later in the afternoon.

Seeing Amber outside with a group of mutual friends, Michelle approached everyone with a lively greeting, and definitely showed off her styled hair.

Amber was polite as always and was sure to compliment Michelle's hair. "Your hair looks nice, Michelle."

"What's that, Amber?"

Amber repeated herself. "I like your hair; it's nice."

Being terribly envious of Amber also included envy towards her natural beauty and her long, brown hair. Michelle's styled, fresh-out-of-the-beauty-salon hair was finally proof that she was superior. As the spoiled child that she was, Michelle harshly replied with a tone a voice that suggested her simple statement to have deeper meaning. "Uh... *Thanks!*"

It was an indicator for Amber to shut down and close up before receiving a dose of verbal and critical abuse.

But Michelle felt her point hadn't been made clearly enough. "Hey Amber, why are you suddenly so quiet?"

"I don't know; I don't have anything to say, I guess."

"Don't have anything to say? Do you know what I think? I think you're jealous of my hair."

It was the most ridiculous thing Amber had heard. "What?" Although she was polite to compliment Michelle's hair moments ago, she secretly felt that it didn't look right on an eleven year old girl, not to mention the over-applied makeup.

"That's right; you're jealous. Who here thinks that Amber is jealous of my hair; just plain jealous of me?"

Somehow, Michelle swayed their mutual friends into her way of thinking as everyone took turns replying, "Me!" Then poor Amber would have to hear her friends proclaim how they truly liked Michelle, and if Amber wasn't a friend of Michelle's, no one would be a friend of Amber's.

Now alone that summer afternoon, Amber angrily sat in her bedroom, gazing from a short distance through the open window that provided a clear view of the activities of Michelle's backyard. How she hated Michelle in that moment, feeling that punishment was long overdue.

Inside Michelle's home, her older brother by five years sat in his bedroom, listening to an audio assault of shrilling death metal that dictated all sorts of acts of violence. He lounged in his comfy chair while relaxing to the soothing music, and reading an article from Soldier of Fortune magazine that described how to make homemade C4 explosives. Where-as most teenage boys hide Playboy magazines under the bed, Danny maintained his hidden stockpile of controversial Soldier of Fortune magazines that were forbidden by Father.

Suddenly, Mother's voice could be heard from downstairs, "Danny? Danny!"

He softly cursed and quickly hid the magazine. Then he ran to the hallway. "What?"

"You need to go outside and start the barbeque!"

Start the barbeque? That was a terrible mistake! Mother was unaware that Danny had the nickname of "Pyro". He had a secret, makeshift shack in the woods where he stockpiled a collection of homemade napalm in old mason jars. Has the reader ever made napalm?—dropping Styrofoam into a jar of gasoline to make a flammable gel that sticks to walls and burns for a long time. Danny was the master of doing this. He would act out his soldier of fortune fantasies by sneaking a jar of napalm to one of the neighborhood parks after dark, and stick it to the playground equipment to be ignited and burned for hours. He once attempted the construction of a pipe bomb by filling a pipe with hundreds of match heads. Fortunately he lacked the technique of effectively sealing the pipe at both ends which would have caused a serious explosion if done properly.

Danny had no reason for his pyromania other than something to wildly decorate his reputation with. He was a rebel without a cause. And on that summer day, he was being asked to start a fire in the barbeque!

Danny cracked a most disturbing smile along with a terribly devious look in his eyes! "Sure Mom!"

Mother continued, "And use the big one, Danny. We've got a lot of guests coming today."

Watching through her window, only Amber was aware of the teenage boy who burst out into the backyard and quickly dragged the large barbeque near the pool where it was nearly overflowed with charcoal.

While this was happening, Danny's sister, Michelle, played a rowdy game with her friends as they chased each other around with water balloons. At some point, little Michelle called out, "Hey, you can't get my hair wet! I just got it done!"

At that moment, Amber thought to herself, "You're going to wish that your hair got wet!" Then she recalled every rude and mean thing Michelle had ever said. Amber let her emotions build up while remaining still and silent. To her, the emotions were flashes of energy that discharged in the air as she began to fantasize with all her heart, wishing for her thoughts to finally come true.

While this happened, Michelle's brother held two bottles of lighter fluid upside-down and heavily sprayed the charcoal, crisscrossing back and forth while calling imaginary people, who lived in the charcoal, obscene names and demanding that they die.

But Danny's game had to be briefly interrupted as the charcoal needed to soak up the lighter fluid. He would return several moments later and drop the bomb on the enemy village.

In the meantime, Amber sat completely motionless and absorbed in flood of harnessed, negative emotions. She maintained a fixed gaze on that little bitch, Michelle, while fantasizing the most horrific tragedy.

One could call the new game between Michelle and her friends, water balloon tag. For you see, Michelle found the perfect gool and it was located at the barbeque. No one could throw water balloons around the barbeque. Of course remaining on gool for too long was no fun! Michelle would soon run away to be further chased by rowdy girls with water balloons.

Sometime later, Danny ran out of the house with a box of matches. He was an expert of making what he called, "fireballs", which involved striking the match against the rough surface of the box while simultaneously flicking it into the air. The end result looked like a projected fireball that continued to burn as it hit the ground.

This "fireball" technique was going to be his missile launched at the enemy village. But before launching from the air, perhaps it was best to add more lighter fluid to ensure that those bastards scorched upon impact.

A responsible adult would have never taken lighting the barbeque to such an extreme measure. Even more, a responsible adult would have never stood six feet away while further drenching the charcoals with fluid. It was in this moment when his younger sister had run past to receive a heavy spray of lighter fluid to her hair.

Michelle was outraged, "Danny!"

"What? Get out of the way, stupid! What are you playing by the barbeque for?"

The other girls weren't outraged like Michelle, and instead whipped a couple water balloons at her. This resumed the desperate game of water balloon tag as Michelle looked for a place to escape. She was still concerned about the heavy amount of lighter fluid sprayed on her head. But she hadn't considered the danger it presented.

And then a "fireball" had been launched that glowed towards the sky and quickly returned to hit the target. While this happened, Michelle ran back to gool for safety. Although Danny may have been six feet from what was about to be an explosion, little Michelle stood one foot away from the barbeque, and was short enough to be even closer to the destruction.

The barbeque nearly exploded with a violent eruption of flames that reached four feet in the air. To make matters worse, upon initial explosion, a wind blew the flames in Michelle's direction so that her entire head and face became engulfed in flames. The combined lighter fluid on her hair and any chemicals used at the beauty salon served as an accelerant that quickly set her head ablaze.

Instinctively, she ran away from the explosion but was soon aware that her head remained on fire. And this wasn't a case of someone's hair simply burning; this was a roaring, twisting flame that violently danced around her head. She screamed in horror, all the while the sizzling and popping of her hair and scalp could be heard.

The brave soldier-of-fortune now ran towards the house in tears to get help. This wasn't supposed to happen! He was responsible for cooking his sister's head, and there would soon be Hell to pay.

But Father saw everything and ran outside. "Jump in the pool! Michelle, jump in the pool!" He ran towards his daughter who was horrified and in shock, obviously confused and not thinking of the sensible thing.

By the time little Michelle had been thrown in the water, her scalp was cooked and included many boils. Only patches of charred strands of hair remained. Finally, justice had been served!

Chapter Two

Amber told no one of what she had done, especially Mother! As Amber saw it, maintaining humility while at the same time radiating a simple beauty as Mother demanded, would sometimes make her a victim to cruel people like Michelle. Surely there would be many times in life that this power needed to be called upon. It was best to keep it a secret from everyone.

And she certainly used this gift plenty of times in high school. Once during a track meet, there was an equaled contender who was worried of losing to Amber. It was best for this girl, Molly, to approach Amber, directly, and let it be known that she would win—not Amber.

Being modest and down-to-earth, Amber merely replied, "Well best of luck to you!" Then she shook Molly's hand.

It wasn't the response Molly anticipated. She came from a family of winners and was full-aware of the winner's attitude. It was confidence that set a winner apart from a loser. This confidence needed to be established with her contender. "Well that's very nice of you to wish me luck. But you know, most people would agree that I have the winner's edge and you don't!"

That was a big mistake on Molly's part! Had she turned and walked away after Amber's wish, she probably would have won the race.

But for Amber, this sudden concept of being a loser, simply because she didn't have the winner's edge, was disturbing. What if Molly was right? Was Amber destined to go through life, losing and never coming out ahead?

Anxiety-driven fantasies of what people truly thought of Amber continued to invade her mind. It wasn't right to be trampled over by winners and then to be laughed at. Ill wishes against Molly that were fueled by ever-expanding, negative emotions were repeated in her mind again and again. It was Molly who did this to her. Molly needed to have something bad happen to her!

Running like never before, ready to take what was rightfully hers, Molly lost control and severely rolled her ankle; not just pulling the ligaments and tendons, but tearing them. It would require surgery and many weeks in a cast, and many more in therapy. Would Molly ever restore her ankle to what it was before? Hopefully her winner's edge would have maintained a positive attitude.

* * *

Holding boys captivated and spellbound is an easy task for any beautiful, young lady. Amber certainly had no need for the gift when it came to her love life. But after graduating high school, she found it very tempting to attract the right sort of guy with her magical charm. But she soon realized that imposing her will and captivating the perfect guy wasn't really true love. As soon as she eased the spell, a certain guy would become distracted and suddenly become attracted to another young lady.

Perhaps it would have been better to cast a milder spell on a desired guy, just enough to sway him into surrendering to his feelings. This is what Amber finally did, and then released the mild spell to test a certain guy's reaction. As luck would have it, the first subject to this experiment stayed with Amber, proving to be true love!

But in all life's cruelty with its twists of irony, Amber's true love left her in a most vulnerable time when Amber needed him most. She had been abandoned; left cold, empty and heartbroken at a most-challenging moment in her life. (More on that later.) Amber could have made him stay simply by focusing all her will until he was madly in love again. But it wouldn't have been true love. Amber knew this. And she suddenly grew tired of pursuing young men her own age.

In that moment, Amber believed herself to be some years wiser than other young women her age. And she was, really; just needed a little fine tuning and some life experience. With her true love gone and realizing that she deserved better, Amber began to call out to an older man who, somewhere, may have been experiencing heartache. Perhaps he was married to an unfaithful wife and was soon to receive divorce papers. Or perhaps he was about to lose his beautiful wife to a tragic accident or sudden illness. Whatever the case, Amber would enter his life with open arms and heal the heartache. He would never leave her, only love and adore Amber forever more.

Over a year passed as Amber played out this emotional fantasy night after night. And then she had awoken one drizzly, Saturday morning in 1994, truly feeling that she somehow bonded or connected with the man who needed her. She gazed out the window and softly whispered, "I'm here for you. Where are you?"

But this morning was not about Amber, despite what she would have believed. This morning was about a man named Michael, who sat in a chair, overlooking his beautiful wife, Linsey, who remained peacefully in dreamland. Her chest would slowly rise and fall under the blankets, a sight that Michael drunk in very deeply as he further imagined Linsey's life-radiating skin receiving circulation and oxygen. Every moment together was precious. In recent months they maintained the practice of sleeping closer than in previous years. They made love a little more, laughed and cried a little more and continued to reaffirm to one another how deep their love was.

Throughout her life, Linsey had natural, strawberry red hair that was worn straight and long below her shoulders. She had fair skin that was nearly transparent enough to reflect more of a pink color. Her eyes were the lightest and vibrant blue that could melt one from a distance just with a momentary glance. And through womanhood, her body had that deliciously curvaceous build to include a barely noticeable cinnamon dusting along the flesh of her chest, shoulders and upper back.

But in the course of a year, Linsey's body deteriorated to a state of being sickly thin and pale to the point of losing her once healthy, pink color. Her eyes remained blue, of course, but they lost the ability to melt with her warm and vibrant gaze. And her long, straight, strawberry, red hair had thinned in many parts, many other areas to be replaced by lifeless, split grays.

In just over a year, Linsey was dying of a mysterious, autoimmune disease for which there was no cure. Her body was aggressively attacking itself; destroying tissue, muscle, organs and even elements of her nervous system. If failing to identifying the cause was not frustrating enough, the typical treatment of immunosupression (medicines that shut down the immune system to prevent further destruction of the body) would only provide a temporary remission. It appeared that Linsey's immune system would build up a tolerance to the medications so that it rebounded with a fury, causing damage far worse than before.

Just like many who are dying of a disease, Linsey had an indomitable spirit that provided her the will to live each day to the fullest. She refused to lie in bed. The disease would certainly kill her, but as Linsey felt, she would not allow her condition to take those final moments of life away.

Although transformed from the woman that Michael once knew, he loved her all the same, and much more! As he sat over her bed that drizzly Saturday morning, Linsey stirred and opened her eyes.

Michael was the first thing seen for the day. "Good morning…" She greeted her loving husband.

"Good morning; were you dreaming?"

She stretched some, "Yeah…"

"I love sitting here watching you sleep. You look so peaceful, like you're having sweet dreams. Linsey, I really wish you would let me have a death mask of you made. I'm going to miss you so terribly when you're gone. The death mask could lie at your pillow and give me comfort, suggesting that you are merely sleeping beside me so peacefully."

Her blue eyes locked on his, "Michael, no! We've been through this before. I don't want a death mask of me made. That's so morbid. And besides; when I'm gone, I won't be laying in this bed. I'll be in a better place, watching over you and Paulette."

Michael didn't want to discuss or be reminded of the times beyond his wife's death. It was better to live in the moment and cherish what they had in the present. He recoiled his wish and simply replied, "As you wish…"

Although possessing an indomitable spirit, Linsey wasn't capable of rising out of bed every morning. There were times when she could hardly move her legs. On a couple occasions, paramedics were summoned because of fear that Linsey was having a heart attack. Again, it was the mysterious, autoimmune disease. Any region of her body could have been under lethal attack. However, in recent times, she was under a state of remission. But like always, Linsey would slowly get out bed in a means to gauge her condition for the day.

Like often, Michael asked, "Are you ready to get up for the day? You can lay there if you want. I'll take care of Paulette and make breakfast for the morning."

"No, I'm fine." Linsey pushed herself up and removed the covers. "I think it'll be easy today." Linsey's feet touched the floor then she stood up.

Michael gently put his hands to Linsey, "Are you alright? Do you need help walking?" Michael would have walked every step if she needed it. He would give half of his life to keep his wife breathing when that sad day finally came.

But this was the line that totally annoyed Linsey. Although kind and sweet, his sappiness was a little overdone. "Michael, I'm fine! Thank you, but I can walk and get ready for the day. Make us some coffee. I'll get Paulette ready and make us breakfast."

By the time that drizzly, Saturday morning in 1994 arrived with Amber calling out to her long-lost lover, Michael brewing up coffee in the kitchen and Linsey entering her daughter's room for the morning; a computer provided much of Paulette's ability to speak. If she had something to say that pseudo-telepathy or charades couldn't communicate, Paulette could poke with a pencil at a keyboard in front of her face to form sentences to express her thoughts, ideas and feelings.

"Good morning!" Mother gave her daughter a warm greeting.

Paulette smiled in acknowledgement to her mother. The keyboard was unnecessary for simple gestures. Aside from that, Paulette was still in bed.

"Are you ready to get up for the day?"

Paulette nodded, yes.

"Okay, let's get you all cleaned up and dressed; then we'll go down to have breakfast." Linsey would never allow her daughter to be neglected. Paulette was not to be an invalid who was left unwashed and stinky for a couple days, wearing frumpy clothes with greasy hair and a stale, crusty mouth. Paulette's hair was always beautiful! She was groomed daily from head-to-toe and she wore all the latest fashions, even had regular manicures and pedicures. Paulette was a beautiful girl and very, much loved by Mother and Father.

Much time was spent between Linsey and her daughter. Being a best friend to Paulette was best. Linsey read her daughter books, magazines of teen pop culture, and was sure to provide the latest music or movies that other teenage girls enjoyed. And although she had a large bedroom with every luxury a child could wish for, and a beautiful walkout turret balcony yielding a gorgeous view of the wilderness below, Paulette was never left alone for lengthy hours. Father was sure to install a wheelchair lift to bring her up and down the stairs.

Once groomed, dressed and ready for the day, Paulette was brought downstairs into the kitchen where Father greeted her, "Good morning, Honey." Then he kissed her softly on the cheek.

On that drizzly, Saturday morning in 1994; Linsey made her family a hearty breakfast of eggs, pancakes and bacon. Tomorrow would be church, followed by a breakfast in town. Saturday was the family's "laid back" day. But before eating, the family was sure hold hands around the table in a moment of prayer, giving thanks for another day together and the many blessings the family shared.

Chapter Three

On a cold, frosty, predawn morning in October, with only the soft glow of pastel ambers glowing in the eastern horizon, Michael stirred from his sleep and glanced at the clock on his nightstand. There was still an hour or so left to sleep. He rolled over to face his beautiful Linsey who lay on her back and deep asleep. It was too tempting not to lay his forearm over her shoulder and lay a kiss on her cheek while breathing in the smell of Linsey's sweet hair.

But then he had to whisper, "You're cold; you need some more covers?" Soon it became evident as to just how cold Linsey really was. She radiated no body heat under the covers and would not stir as Michael slowly rubbed his palm on her arms, her abdomen or thigh. "Linsey?" The slow caresses that were intended to warm and stir his sleeping beauty increased to a frantic diagnostic check. Now he spoke out in a regular tone of voice, "Linsey?"

Michael switched on his nightstand light and stood up. A flush of panic surged through his body as he quickly walked around to where Linsey lay. He violently pushed at Linsey's side of the mattress, "Linsey?"

Her chest did not rise or fall; nor was there the sound of deep, sleep-full breathing or twitching of her eyes to suggest being spellbound by a REM.

Still, Michael had to call out while attempting to shake his wife awake. "Linsey!"

She was stiff and very cold. At some point in the night her heart must have stopped beating. In recent weeks the summer's remission appeared to have ended as Linsey suddenly became gravely ill.

Although men certainly get choked up or glass at the eyes in an emotional moment, men rarely cry. And every man can recall the very, last time in boyhood that he attempted to weep or sob. But that moment often ends up in laughter as a young man asks himself, "What the hell am I doing?"

Perhaps the fact that men rarely cry is the reason why the sight of a grown man, who has fallen to pieces and weeps uncontrollably, can be disturbing. Michael kneeled before his beloved Linsey with his upper body draped over her chest in uncontrollable sobs. Then he raised his head as if gazing at the ceiling. But in those moments, one sees beyond the confines of walls and plaster and can gaze into the endless void where Heaven, somewhere, might be found.

He continued to sob until words were finally possible. "An angel must have taken you sometime in the night..." Warm, heavy tears ran down his cheeks. Then he looked back down at his lifeless Linsey, "But you look to be only sleeping..."

It was still so early in the morning. Paulette would surely be sleeping for another hour or two. It would give Michael the small window of time that was needed to keep a memory and reminder of those sweet moments when he watched his Linsey peacefully sleep.

Her long, beautiful hair was pulled back and a bandana from the lingerie drawer was slipped over the top of her head to protect it. Next, a thin layer of petroleum jelly was rubbed into Linsey's beautiful face and underneath her jaw line. The petroleum jelly would serve as protection to the skin, but needed to be a thin layer so that any natural lines or cracks that were barely noticeable of Linsey's mature face would be remembered.

In the garage, hidden in a dark corner of a cabinet, were a box of dry Plaster of Paris and two rolls of Plaster of Paris gauze strips. Michael quietly descended the stairs and carefully opened the exterior door to the attached garage to get those items that he thought would never be used. Back into the house, he softly entered the kitchen and filled two bowls with warm water, and then added the proper amount of dry Plaster of Paris. It was necessary to be extra quiet when ascending the stairs, as Paulette certainly could not be awoken!

Standing at Linsey's nightstand, strips of Plaster of Paris gauze were cut in equal lengths, dipped in the plaster mixture, and then added to the perimeter of Linsey's face. Once fully perimeter with the edges blended in, additional gauze strips were added so that her entire face was soon covered. The setting time would only take fifteen to twenty minutes. But while this was done, Michael checked to ensure that his daughter was sleeping.

In a rare occurrence, Paulette was awake! But she couldn't be alarmed of her mother's passing just yet. Father hid his grief and simply greeted his daughter, "Good morning, Honey. Are you up already?"

Paulette nodded.

"Your Mother is not doing well this morning. We're going to have to…" He closed his eyes in what could have been interpreted as a prolonged blink and then continued, "…let her rest and then see how she's doing."

Paulette stared at her father, which indicated a need for something.

"What is it, Honey? Do you need to use the bathroom? Of course; I'll get your wheelchair."

Paulette quickly shook her head, "no" while making grunts. Then she looked at the keyboard.

It was best for Michael to respect his daughter's wish and wheel the computer and keyboard over to her bed. He lifted and supported the paralyzed girl so that she could sit up and type a sentence into the keyboard by poking it with a pencil.

"I want to see Mom."

"Honey, your Mother is not awake. She's not doing well this morning."

Her eyes filled with tears. Then she poked a simple word into the keyboard, "Please!" Paulette knew the worse had happened. Maybe she heard her Father sobbing in the other room behind closed doors. Perhaps she was aware of the stirring around downstairs and some activity taking place in the bedroom. Whatever it was, Paulette knew something was wrong.

But Michael couldn't let his daughter see Linsey just yet. The Plaster of Paris had yet to dry. It would be another fifteen minutes before the mask set, and even longer to clean the petroleum jelly and restore her appearance to undisturbed. "Okay, Honey. Give me a few minutes and I'll bring you to your mother."

Every minute that passed while waiting for the plaster to dry was another moment of dishonesty to his daughter. The mask could not come off fast enough when finally set. But the petroleum jelly was quite a challenge to remove. Who sleeps with that mess applied to the face?

By the time Michael returned to Paulette's room, she wore a face of severe disappointment. She wasn't stupid. She knew that a few minutes shouldn't have evolved into nearly an hour. What was Father's problem?

"Okay, sorry for the holdup. Let's take you in to see your mother." Paulette was lifted out of bed and gently set in the wheelchair. Then Michael knelt before his daughter while holding her hands. "Paulette, there's something I need to tell you."

Paulette's eyes glassed, knowing what would be heard next.

"Your mother has passed away…"

Paulette let out a cry. Forming intelligible words is unnecessary when expressing such deep sadness. All creatures cry; it's instinctive.

"I'm so sorry, Honey. I needed some time; please understand."

The wheelchair was rolled out of the bedroom, down the hall and into Mother and Father's bedroom. There on the bed lay the lifeless body of not only the girl's mother, but a best friend who kept Paulette living and feeling like a real person in all those years existing as a vegetable. Who would Paulette have now? Father certainly loved Paulette, but who would replace the person who loved her in only the way a mother could?

Chapter Four

Small, rural towns like Sillmac and Mapleview often carry over traditions from the days when immigrant settlers lived closely like family. In those days, farming, hunting, gathering and building homes were often community projects. Together, the community of olden times learned to survive in the harshest of conditions. In those days, people needed one another. Independence and a need for solitude were never an option.

And when a member of the community passed away, the entire town gathered for the funeral and then a dinner. Everyone brought a dish to pass around. You certainly wouldn't expect the grieving family to cook for the entire town! In those moments, love and a shared meal were needed.

In modern times, Mapleview and surrounding areas maintain the old customs of funerals. The entire town gathers for a funeral and then meets for dinner at either the church hall, or a reception hall. Of course no one expects the grieving family to provide dinner for the entire town! People bring a sizable platter of their family specialties, a potluck dinner.

There is one thing that the grieving family provides during the dinner. It's an unusual tradition in which the grieving family orders bacon from the popular Saulmon's Meats of Mapleview. Saulmon's is a family owned business that has been passed down for many generations. Originally a shack in the 1800s that cured meats and butchered kill from a hunt, the business grew to what it is today and now operates in a modern storefront. Saulmon's Meats continues to provide butchering services; but the current owner in 1994, Curt Saulmon, Sr.—his son to be next in line to owning and operating the business—added to the establishment so that it sold various sausages, ham, bacon and jerky.

Although grieving the recent loss of his beautiful Linsey and faced with a funeral to plan, Michael did own the chain of hardware stores that was rapidly appearing in every town of America. He definitely had more money than he knew what to do with! I mean the guy purchased a small mountain in Sillmac and had a castle-like mansion built on top. He certainly didn't need the town to bring family dishes to share at Linsey's funeral. But local customs and traditions were always followed. Aside from that, nobody wanted to eat generic chicken, beef and spaghetti from a reception hall. Everyone was proud of their family recipes, and everyone wished to share and sample. They wanted big pots of chili, sweet sauerkraut cooked in bacon grease, homemade dumplings, Belgian trippe, numerous casseroles and a vast array of homemade deserts. Funerals were serious business in the Mapleview area! It was best for Michael to step aside and let the town feed the guests and family. But he was sure to reserve the finest reception hall, provide plenty of Saulmon's bacon and treat family and guests to an open bar.

It isn't necessary to provide the details of Linsey's sad, sad funeral. It was just as any other funeral: the worse day ever for a spouse, any children, parents and siblings. Hysterical tears and close embraces marked the final departure.

But it's more interesting to discuss the way in which Michael spent his days prior to the wake and funeral. With Linsey's body being prepared at the Grossenbury funeral home in Mapleview, Michael began and completed phase two and three of the dedicated death mask to the love of his life.

Michael was never an artist, much less a sculptor. Aside from following the simple instructions of making a death mask, he struggled with improvising the proper technique in developing Linsey's face into a sculpted head. Surely it should have been as simple as to fill the curved inside of the mask with clay until the form of a head was finally achieved. But consider how delicate the initial application of clay needed to be. Too much applied pressure while packing the clay against the inside of the face would have caused a break. This would have been nearly as devastating as losing Linsey, herself.

With her face padded by numerous soft cloths and gently set against the mattress of their bed; small pieces of clay, no larger than the diameter of Michael's thumbprint, were carefully applied to the inside one piece at a time. His moistened finger gently smoothed the clay against the surface before applying another small piece. It was a grueling, tedious and highly time-consuming task. As the hours passed while Michael feared breaking the death mask, he could feel Linsey's spirit overlooking, watching in outrage that her husband had gone against her wishes. Perhaps she would have been able to influence the mask to break.

To avoid this, Michael spoke out to his deceased wife. "Linsey, I am so sorry for doing this. Please understand. I know you understand how important this is to me. You'll see just how beautiful you'll look when the work is finally complete."

Paulette needed her father in this moment. She was left alone for a few hours at a time while Father painstakingly filled Linsey's face. Linsey, herself, urged Michael through subliminal means to put the silly project down and focus on what was more important. What was left of their family strongly needed closeness and sharing of feelings. Instead, Michael continued to bring that statue-head to life.

By the time the face's interior was one-third full of clay; Michael felt safe creating flat blankets of clay and laying them along the inside. This reduced the time for filling the remains of Linsey's face and allowed for rests to spend more time with Paulette.

A day before Linsey's wake, the entire face had been filled and hardened with clay. The final step was to merely roll a large ball of clay that could be sliced in such a way that it would be attached to her face and serve as the remainder of the head. Linsey would have hair, so not much detail was required for the top and back of her head.

There wasn't time to paint the face! Although Michael wished to have flesh-colored paint along with a hint of Linsey's blush, and perhaps some color to her lips, the materials used for this would have needed to be tested and may have taken many hours to prove effective. The wrong color or tone of paint would have been a disaster. Again, it was important for that head to look *exactly* the way Linsey looked when alive.

There was still enough time to apply her long, strawberry-red hair. But where would he find Linsey's hair? Michael announced to his daughter that he would go to Saulmon's Meats and pick up the bacon for the funeral. The girl had been left alone before, but only for about a half hour at a time. Little did Paulette know that in addition to picking up the bacon, Father would also venture about an hour away to an adult entertainment store that sold toys and costumes. A wig of long, strawberry-red hair would be the finishing touches to Linsey's head that was needed before the funeral.

* * *

Mapleview and the surrounding area make up a population of perhaps nearly 200,000 people. Surely the population of Mapleview and Sillmac wouldn't go to every funeral. How could you fit that many people into a church or a reception hall? Stating that the entire town attends a funeral is merely a statement made to imply that old customs are still followed. The truth is, just about everyone stays home or at work (depending on the day of the week). The lives of strangers aren't interrupted for funerals that happen throughout the week. But the custom continues to be followed by senior citizens, officials of churches, political figures, police and fire personnel or influential members of the community. And this is no freeloader society! Everyone brings a special dish to share. Think of the after-funeral dinner as a friendly open house where people can socialize, network or develop their public image for the next election.

It might be someone like Jack Swieley whose residential brokerage company was rapidly taking off in Mapleview. Oh… I suppose Jack Swieley might have been considered a freeloader! He brought nothing to share with family and guests of Linsey's funeral. But attending a funeral in town guaranteed a good, hearty meal along with the chance to meet grieving family who might be planning on selling their home. Mr. Swieley would never offer his card or ask for business on a day like this! He would merely identify himself as broker Jack Swieley from Jack Swieley Realty. Chances are family would remember the nice man who extended his condolences, and telephone him some months later when thinking of selling.

Another guest who attended Linsey's funeral and dinner was Loraine Trivelli, who was young enough in 1994 to hopefully be noticed by the handsome and very, wealthy Michael Dickly. Loraine was an influential member of the community, as she was owner of the historic Trivelli house in Mapleview. Accompanying Loraine on that day was her sister and young niece, Mary, who was a young lady of only fourteen-years-old. Mary would one day purchase the historic house from her aunt so that she and her future husband could settle down. Of course Loraine and her sister weren't a couple of freeloaders! They were sure to have brought two pans of homemade chocolate chip coconut bars to share with everyone.

Before everyone would be invited to help themselves to food, Michael carried a box up to a podium that sat on an elevated portion of the floor. Then he spoke into the microphone which immediately quieted the room. A grieving husband who speaks at his deceased wife's funeral dinner was not a common occurrence.

Being president of Dickly's Hardware and addressing groups of people at meetings or conventions was second nature for Michael. "Ladies and gentlemen, I first want to thank everyone for joining our family, today. It's been a very, sad week; not only for Paulette and myself, but Linsey's parents, two brothers and the rest of her family. But thank you for coming out, extending your sympathies and sharing your family recipes. I can't wait to try what everyone has brought. Keep in mind it's an open bar, and look: I was sure to bring plenty of Saulmon's bacon!"

The entire room laughed in reply. The bacon was a silly tradition, but always followed.

Michael continued, "I want to share with you something I had worked on throughout the week. Needless to say, the loss of Linsey has deeply affected me. I had a death mask made of Linsey..." Michael opened the box and carefully pulled out Linsey's statue-head. Then he set it on the podium.

Paulette looked up from her wheelchair in horror as tears streamed down her cheeks. Had Father lost his mind? How could he have done such a thing?

Michael continued, "Then I continued filling her face with clay, formed a head and added the hair. The end product now sits up here with me. As you can see, she looks to be only sleeping; but she's here with us in spirit." Michael kissed his wife on the forehead. "She's not completely finished. I want to color her face so that she looks exactly how I remember her. She is very important to me. I hope you all like my work."

There were a couple seconds of silence before broker Jack Swieley stood up from his seat and announced, "It's beautiful!"

He clapped his hands, eager to get everyone else to applaud so that eating could finally begin. Soon every followed, including family—everyone, that is, but Paulette and the immediate family on Linsey's side.

Linsey remained on the podium throughout dinner. The word dinner is used, but really it was a huge luncheon served at one o'clock in the afternoon. People continued to fill up on Swedish meatballs over egg noodles, slow-cooked cocktail wieners in barbeque sauce, spaetzle, homemade pierogies with polish sausage (from Saulmon's), hearty chili and stews; the list just went on! And there was plenty of drinking, too! Linsey's funeral was a big success. But there was one event that had yet to take place.

While Michael appeared to be finishing a conversation at the food table, a beautiful, young lady with long, light-brown hair carefully approached with her eyes deeply set onto Michael. He froze while she approached. The noise in the room was suddenly far off in the distance, barely heard. The young woman stuck out her hand while asking, "Mr. Dickly?"

He quickly answered while taking her hand, "Yes!"

"I'm so sorry. I read the obituary in the paper and was deeply touched. I feel so bad for you and your daughter… Oh excuse me, I'm Amber."

Michael continued to hold her hand, "Nice to meet you, Amber."

While this happened, Loraine Trivelli brought another plate of food to the table and announced while sitting down next to Mary, "They have Belgian trippe from Saulmon's! I brought a couple over."

Loraine's sister gladly took one. But Mary wasn't fond of Belgian trippe, a sausage made with cabbage. The Belgian sausage smelled like a backed-up sewer, but certainly didn't taste the same. Still, the young Mary wasn't about to try one.

Suddenly, Loraine saw Amber talking to the handsome and wealthy Michael Dickly. Their eyes remained locked on one another while maintaining a prolonged handshake. "Do you see that?" asked Loraine. "Let me tell you; I don't like that young lady one bit! Look how she talks to him on the day of his wife's funeral. She's up to no good if you ask me! Seems like a nice, young lady; but…"

She was quickly interrupted by the young Mary, "Oh, she's fine, Aunt Loraine. She's only extending her sympathies."

Amber knew in her heart that Michael was the one she had connected with for so many nights. But was he aware that she was the new destiny? And was he open to the young woman who would receive him with open arms and an ability to heal the heartache? That day was a simple test. Amber needed to verify what she felt in her heart was true. And this is why the young woman had the courage and audacity to suddenly announce to her soon-to-be soul mate, "I just want you to know that I suffered a broken heart, too. If you ever need a friend, or just someone to talk to, sort through your feelings…"

Suddenly, Linsey's statue-head toppled over on the podium! Gasps could be heard from those in the room. In a panic, Michael quickly pulled away from Amber's hand and nearly flew up to the elevated portion of the floor and to the podium, where he rescued his beautiful wife.

Michael gently picked up Linsey and verified that no damage had been done. Then he asked, "Are you alright? I'm so sorry; you've had such an eventful day. It's best to put you away and bring you home where we can rest tonight."

The statue was placed in the box and away from everyone's view.

* * *

Taking Linsey's advice from earlier in the week, Michael now made a conscious effort to give Paulette extra attention now that her mother was gone. Michael was wrong to have neglected her so much while preparing for Linsey's funeral. Later in the evening, hours after the funeral, father and daughter sat downstairs in the family room, seated side-by-side on the sofa. Paulette wasn't always confined to the wheelchair. She often lay on the grass outside on warm, summer days with Mother. Sometimes she sat up in her comfy, beanbag chair while watching videos with Mother and Father. And tonight she cuddled up next to Father with his arm around her.

Father said, "I'm really sorry about the way I acted earlier in the week. I was overwhelmed with sadness and had to make sure your mother's funeral went according to plan. I was wrong, and I totally admit it. Honey, I promise that I'll never leave you neglected. You and I need to get closer. We're the only thing we've got right now. I've actually considered selling Dickly's to some other company, selling this castle and buying a small house for you and me to live in. I have so much money that I never need to work again. And when I'm gone, there would be plenty of money for you. We'll just have to find a way for you to have some degree of independence."

A tear from Paulette dripped onto Michael's shoulder. It had been an emotionally draining week for the girl, and hearing Father announce such dedication was very much needed.

And then they sat for a while until Paulette fell asleep. Michael lifted his baby, carried her up the flight of stairs and tucked her in bed. With a gentle kiss to her cheek he whispered, "Good night, Honey. I love you."

It was time for Michael to retire as well. Entering his bedroom, he could see that Linsey was already sound asleep. He changed into his sleepwear and slipped into bed. Then he kissed his beautiful wife on the lips. "You've had such an eventful day. Oh, but your funeral was beautiful. So many people came. And

I'm sorry for leaving you out on the podium like that. But we're home now."

Michael pulled closer to Linsey's side of the bed and breathed in deeply the smell of his wife's pillows. "Oh, Linsey; I don't know what I'm going to do. You need to help me; you need to help me figure out how to take care of our girl. Should I sell the business and move in a small house? It seems like the logical thing to do. But the business can grow larger and make us more money." Tears ran from Michael's eyes, "Please help me, Linsey. Don't leave me alone down here."

Take away the morbid presence of Linsey's death mask; Michael's behavior wouldn't have been considered so odd. Many a grieving husband or wife has laid on a spouse's side of the bed while asking for help and speaking out to be heard in Heaven.

Chapter Five

It was somewhere around a quarter-past four o'clock in the afternoon the following day. Michael and Paulette sat in the family room throughout much of the afternoon as Father flipped through the TV channels and watched random programming. A candle sat on one of the side tables next to a recent photo of Linsey. Those in mourning have found that candles offer a sense of comfort. Burning them throughout the home would be the new practice for Michael and his daughter.

The question of, "What shall we have for dinner?" replayed a couple of times in Michael's mind. It was still too early to eat, but Michael suspected that his daughter wondered the same. The usual practice in the Mapleview area is for the grieving family to take home all the food from the funeral and eat it throughout the week. But Michael felt it more appropriate to donate the large remains to the homeless shelters. He had more money than he knew what to do with, and didn't feel right accepting more food than he needed.

Linsey had made her divine manicotti on the night before she died. There was still half a pan in the refrigerator. There is nothing wrong with eating something made by a person who is no longer alive. Michael loved his wife; Paulette loved her mother. And both would agree that Linsey's manicotti was to… well, it shouldn't be put that way; not in this moment. But it would surely be the last time that both would enjoy something made by Linsey.

Amber hadn't given up! She knew in her heart that she and Michael shared a destiny. The test from yesterday only failed because the statue-head of Linsey had toppled over. Amber knew that if this hadn't happened, Michael would have exchanged contact information with her. He needed a special friend; he needed *her* at that moment.

Although failing to exchange contact information, Amber simply found Michael's address in the local phone book. His name was posted right there in alphabetical order to include his telephone number and address. And as she ascended his spiraling driveway that afternoon to the top of the miniature mountain, not one bit of her felt out of place. There was no hesitation or a need to turn around. Amber parked her modest Chevy Cavalier into the horseshoe driveway and stepped out to stand before the enormous castle-like mansion. She reached back into the car and pulled out a large pan of food from the passenger seat, still warm, and ready to be eaten.

Pressing the doorbell triggered a lovely melody of bells. Amber recognized the combination but couldn't place the song in her mind. Linsey always loved Moonlight Sonata, and was ecstatic that her doorbell could produce the combination. In a way, it was Linsey who initially greeted Amber at the door.

Michael opened the door and stood for a split-second as he placed the beautiful, young woman in his mind.

Amber spoke first, "Mr. Dickly?"

"Yes... Amber, from yesterday! Come in!" He could immediately see that a tray of food was being offered and took it. "Oh, and it's still warm. You just cooked it?"

"Yes, it's braciole."

As Amber entered the home, Michael placed the tray of braciole on a large table that sat in the foyer. Then he took her coat. "Please, stay a while."

While Michael hung the young woman's coat in the guest closet, Amber took notice of the beautiful, marble tile that lay along the grand foyer and the enormous, crystal chandelier that hung over the balcony and foyer. And from what she could see, although heavily furnished, the home remained dramatically spacious. "You have a lovely home, Mr. Dickly."

"Please, call me Michael."

In the family room, Paulette struggled to turn her head enough to see the visitor. Michael immediately noticed this and motioned Amber to follow. "Come meet my daughter, Paulette."

As Father and the visitor came closer, they walked at a diagonal, which soon allowed Paulette to look upon Amber with both eyes. Amber had the sudden suspicion that the girl was aware of her intention.

Michael spoke, "Paulette, you probably didn't get a chance to meet Amber at the funeral. But she brought us dinner tonight."

Amber smiled, "Hi, nice to meet you." She stuck out her hand, but then slowly put it down upon realizing Paulette's condition.

Michael needed to further facilitate the introduction, "Paulette is unfortunately paralyzed from the neck, down. She had a bad accident as a little girl and suffered a head injury that took away her ability to speak. Go ahead and shake her hand; just pull it up for her."

Amber took the girl's hand and repeated her greeting, "Hi Paulette, nice to meet you."

Paulette smiled in return.

Michael continued as Amber gently put Paulette's hand back on her lap. "She's fully aware of her surroundings and can communicate. Usually she talks by poking a pencil at a computer keyboard and spells out sentences. But if you pay close attention and slow down, you can almost hear her thoughts. Usually I simply guess what it is she wishes to say, and Paulette nods yes or no. I'm almost always correct in interpreting her expressions."

"Wow, that's amazing."

"She's an amazing girl." was Michael's immediately reply. Then he spoke about dinner. "I was just thinking of what to have for dinner before you came. It's still a little early for us, but I would like you to stay. Can I put the tray of food in the oven under a low temperature to keep it warm?"

"Sure, and I'd love to stay for dinner; that is if it's okay with Paulette."

Paulette nodded and smiled, reassuring Amber that she was welcome.

Michael never heard of the dish that Amber made. "I'm sorry, what did you say we are having for dinner?"

"Braciole; it's my mother's recipe."

"Is that beef… chicken…?"

"It's beef."

"Well I'll go down into the wine cellar and find something red. We'll drink that before dinner. In the meantime, make yourself at home."

Michael walked back into the foyer, picked up the tray and pulled the aluminum back. Underneath were a dozen beef strips that were rolled up, and appeared to have some seasoning, breadcrumbs and cheese in the middle. Surrounding the dozen beef roulades were potatoes that had been sliced in half. "Mm-mmm! Paulette, you are really going to like this!"

Amber called back from across the family room, "Sorry, but I didn't make a vegetable."

"That's okay; we've got bags of tossed salad in the refrigerator. This is plenty!"

Just about everyone has had braciole. Every country has its own variation, and every mother has made it for dinner once or twice. My own wife takes a round steak, flattens it out with a hammer and then slices it into roll-able strips. Then she adds stuffing and some seasonings, browns it in a pan, then lowers the heat to add a gravy made with cream of mushroom soup. The final product is slow cooked for about an hour. It's good stuff!

Other recipes might involve something similar to what Amber made to include a cheese filling. There are veal roulades stuffed with fruits and vegetables. There is even a beef roulade that is stuffed with bacon and pickles.

The way to a man's heart is through his stomach. If you really want to win a man's heart, you should make some nice braciole; served with a hearty, bold, red wine. It'll be just a taste of what your soon-to-be-man can expect when finally surrendering to you.

Now alone with Paulette, Amber felt it was best to strike up conversation. The most important thing was certainly mentioned first. "So, I'm really sorry about your mother."

It was almost as if Paulette's eyes had responded a gratitude for Amber's sympathy.

"Can I sit down?"

Paulette nodded.

"Yeah, I read the obituary in the paper and just felt really bad. I couldn't help but introduce myself to your father."

There was no reason for Amber to cover her intention. Paulette knew the underlying cause for making dinner and visiting. And really she didn't mind. Amber appeared courteous and thoughtful, maybe just the person Father needed as he was certainly too young to give up on life. But was Amber real? Was the person on display the true Amber? This was Paulette's greatest concern.

There was a long pause as Amber realized her intentions were clearly visible to the girl. Then she continued, "There's just something about your father. I felt like I should help."

* * *

Perhaps you are a major opponent to anything that contains alcohol. If so, I suppose you are outraged to read that a person might have a wine cellar in his home. For the rest of us, especially those who enjoy wine, drinking wine is a wonderful experience that has a tendency to even out emotions, open conversation and open doors to newer possibilities. It isn't a terrible thing to enjoy wine with company shortly after the loss of a loved one. No one is getting drunk, just sharing a moment with the dearly departed that remains nearby.

Opening a bottle that blended imported Malbec with Merlot, Michael began to speak of the remaining cases of Pinot Noir that was enjoyed by Linsey. Pinot Noir was always her favorite. Michael was sure to order cases of her favorite, imported wine; various names and blends from vineyards from around the world. But they rightfully belonged to Linsey. He couldn't drink them or give them away just yet. For now, they would sit in the wine cellar.

In recent years, Paulette was permitted on occasion to enjoy wine with Mother and Father. She was usually given just under a glass's amount. Again, she wasn't getting drunk; just enjoying the moment under a mild influence of euphoria. With all she had been through, it was a small taboo that Mother and Father allowed the teenager to have.

In that moment, Michael sat beside his daughter, raising the glass to her lips so she could share what Father and the guest enjoyed. Wine has an interesting effect. It has a tendency to remove some unseen veil between this world and the other. When drunk in moderation, our senses remain intact. Paulette remained on a heightened state of awareness while keenly in tune with the conversation and body language between Father and Amber. Although listening attentively to every word of Michael's, Amber was subliminally seducing the man.

Finished with what remained in his wine glass, Michael set his glass on the table and stood up. "Well, I suspect that the wine is making us all hungry. Is everyone ready to eat?"

"Sure!" replied Amber.

Paulette eagerly nodded.

The table was set; the salad mix was poured in a bowl, and Michael went back down into the wine cellar for another bottle of blended Malbec and Merlot.

Throughout dinner, Michael spoke about the many cruises that the family had taken and the places that Linsey enjoyed most. Michael boasted that year after year, Linsey insisted on hosting the holidays and would spare nothing to make the celebration better than the last. It was such easy conversation for Amber. All she needed to do was listen, and encourage Michael to tell more.

But at some point, the conversation suddenly changed direction. "So what about you, Amber? Are you in school? Maybe recently graduated?"

Amber hated lying! As is the case with most of us, many people had been dishonest throughout Amber's life. She despised people who simply exaggerated or, even worse, spoke wicked lies of deception. And perhaps in this sense, you are very, much like Amber. But ask yourself; was there a brief moment when you lied, today? If you are truthful with yourself, you will admit that there was a moment in which a white lie was spoken.

The fact is lying is an uncontrollable flaw of human nature. Most people do everything in their power to be truthful. But sometimes a white lie is spoken to cover some mild shortcoming or silly error made. It's often done for a good cause. But it's still lying. Perhaps this is partially the reason why we attend church on Sunday. No human is perfect.

Amber's collection of white lies had been rehearsed for some hours before the meeting. She felt that the lies had good intentions and would soon blow away once winning Michael's heart. Although her father was a wealthy man who would have sent his daughter to whatever university accepted her, Amber wasn't fully prepared for a higher education after high school. You cannot force a young woman like Amber to follow a pre-decided path. For a few years after high school, she pretty much did nothing.

In recent times, however, Amber decided to better herself and take general education classes at the Sillmac Community College. Through time, she hoped to find a major.

Amber's white lies were far, more interesting and something for Michael to seriously consider. "I'm taking classes down at the Sillmac Community College, majoring in physical therapy, caring for elderly or handicapped. I hope to one day work with people who have physical limitations."

Michael was impressed, "Really? How's that going?"

"Pretty good… I don't know; I might have to take a break for a while and save up more money. My dad makes just enough money to disqualify for student financial aid for me."

Michael interrupted, "Ah, your Dad is in that middle class range that is unfairly denied financial assistance for his kids' college. He probably makes good money, but it's all used on family and household expenses. See, if he was at the poverty level, or if you were a minority, you would have a free ride through college. If your father was one of the wealthy few in this nation, he could pay out of pocket for your schooling. But for the rest of this country, people have to struggle their way through paying for college. It's funny how the middle class get's the shit-end of the stick—if you pardon my French."

"Oh, yeah! I know all about it!" More lies spoken by Amber! "And I get part time jobs, but they don't pay very well. Plus they only cut into my studies, you know?"

Michael nodded in agreement, appearing to be in contemplation.

For Paulette, it was the most pathetic tale of irony she had ever heard. What was Amber doing, looking for a job? Paulette grew increasingly curious of this visitor.

Some time passed as the visit was nearing its end. For Michael, it was a desperate moment in which he knew that all hinged on his consummation. But how would it look to Paulette? And was it the best thing for his girl? Finally he spoke his suggestion. "Amber… I don't want you to take time off from school. If you can work it into your schedule, I just might have a job for you. I'm sure it's no secret that I'm founder and owner of Dickly's Hardware; you know, the hardware stores springing up all over the nation? I've got a business to operate and can't leave it unattended. But Paulette and I are in a difficult moment. Who can take care of her throughout the day? I'm usually home, but spend many hours in teleconference calls or working on presentations and stuff. How would you like to do a little internship? You major in working with handicapped. I would pay you handsomely if you accepted this offer."

Amber paused, appearing to consider the offer. "Well, it all depends on how Paulette feels about this."

And just how did Paulette feel of the arrangement? Well, let's just say that Paulette was most curious of the woman who suddenly had control over Father.

* * *

Later that night, Michael slipped into bed and moved close to Linsey. "I know what you're thinking. She reminds me so much of you when we first met. And maybe I did give in for a brief moment to those feelings. But Paulette and I need her. You saw her; so considerate of Paulette and seems to have a good head on her shoulders. I'll be home while she's here and will be sure to keep an eye on things. I want to sell the business, but it could take months, maybe a year or two for everything to happen. If I leave it neglected, it'll lose value."

Michael kissed his wife's forehead then sighed. "Listen to me, not being completely open and honest with you. Linsey it's just… well, she really brightened up the evening for us. She just showed up at the front door and was like a God-send."

Chapter Six

This would be a highly challenging week for Amber; not because she accepted a job that she knew nothing about, and not because it would require her to blow off classes at the community college; but because there was more about her life that was kept secret from Michael and Paulette.

It was seven o'clock, Monday morning; not more than twelve hours after her initial dinner with Michael and Paulette. Amber knocked at the door of the Dickly castle.

Shortly after, Michael answered. "Hey, good morning!"

"Good morning!"

"Paulette might still be sleeping. I have coffee if you need some."

"No, I'm fine."

"You sure?"

"Yeah, I'm okay."

Michael took the young woman's coat. Amber looked just as beautiful as the previous evening and caused an immediate, painful yearning for Linsey. Michael covered his longing by suggesting to start the day.

"Well, I suppose we should go upstairs and see if Paulette's awake."

As the two approached and ascended the stairs, Michael nearly apologized for the previous evening. "Listen, I hope I wasn't out of place for suddenly offering this job to you. I guess I'm just desperate, really need someone to care for Paulette."

Amber reassured him, "No, believe me; you are doing me a favor. I'm glad to help."

They were careful in approaching Paulette's bedroom and opening the door, just in case she was still sleeping. But Paulette was awake and waiting to begin her day. Of course Michael wasn't going to immediately turn his daughter over to Amber. He was sure to properly instruct the new caretaker of how to get Paulette out of bed and into the wheelchair. It isn't necessary to provide details on every messy aspect of handling a paralyzed person in those early morning hours. But Amber was given thorough training of those duties, how to operate the crane-like machine that would lower Paulette onto the toilet, and how to keep her supported while she did her business.

Paulette was to be bathed and groomed every morning. Needless to say, undressing the girl was a delicate matter. Michael was relieved to finally have a woman caretaker who could tend to this ritual that was a bit uncomfortable between father and daughter.

While filling the bathtub, Michael urged, "And please; always remember not to fill with too much water. If she happens to slide under, she might drown. I don't know how strong you are; but promise me you won't overfill the tub!"

"I promise I'll be extra careful with her."

Michael continued, "We brush her teeth while she's in the tub. And she likes to use mouthwash. Just bring the bottle up to her lips so she can take a swig. And use a cup so she can spit it out. I'll leave everything over here on the sink."

Paulette was lowered in the bathtub with the crane-like machine. "Do you think you can wash her? I'm sure Paulette is quite finished with Daddy washing her; right, Honey?"

Paulette only returned a blank stare.

"I'll go downstairs and fix breakfast for all of us. Yell downstairs if you need anything."

Alone with Paulette who only gazed up with an unsure look, Amber sat down on the edge of the bathtub for her first heart-to-heart talk with the girl. "I know this must be awkward for you. I'm not much older than you are, and… Well, I'm a stranger to you, I know. I guess I just felt this calling, like I'm supposed to be here and help." Amber's eyes glassed as she stammered in a second of controlling a teardrop. "If you just give me a chance, I can be your friend. I know you and your mother were close friends. Your father didn't tell me this, but I can see it. You need someone to continue that friendship in addition to taking care of you."

Amber took the small bucket and carefully dumped water on Paulette's hair. "It's not going to be easy; there will be some challenges. And it'll take time for you to trust me, I know."

Amber was a quick learner! Much to Michael's surprise, by the time he finished making breakfast, his daughter was not only cleaned for the day; but dressed, seated in the wheelchair and having her hair blow-dried by Amber.

Amber received adequate instruction on how to operate the wheelchair lift so that Paulette could come downstairs. Amber was certainly welcome to enjoy breakfast with Michael and Paulette; but as a caretaker, she was first expected to feed the paralyzed girl until she had eaten her fill. It wasn't necessary for Michael to voice this. In fact, Amber was proactive in feeding Paulette before Michael even thought of asking.

* * *

And this was pretty much the schedule for the first few days: an easy job of simply washing, grooming and dressing Paulette for the morning; bringing her downstairs for breakfast and feeding her; then spending the day with her. One could have thought of Amber as a friend for hire.

But there was a little problem back at home, a small conflict between mother and daughter that Amber tried so gracefully to extinguish every night. It would begin as Amber returned home each day, after her eight hours at the Dickly castle.

"Where have you been all day?"

"School, Mom! Remember, I'm taking classes?" These were more white lies spoken by Amber. They were all for a good cause.

"But you're only going part time!"

"Mom, I need to study and do projects! I've got midterms coming up!"

Mother knew better! Taking part-time general education classes at the Sillmac Community College would not require Amber to leave at 6:30 in the morning and come home close to four o'clock in the afternoon. Amber was probably with a boy, probably the same boy who left her, heartbroken, over a year ago. She was probably out gallivanting with him throughout the day. Mother would put an end to this.

"Amber, I am not going to take care of your daughter while you run around out there. Do you think I was born yesterday? Don't insult my intelligence like that!"

Yes, Amber was a young mother; her one-year-old daughter, Trista, left fatherless because the young man was not ready to accept responsibility. And neither was Amber in Mother's eyes. Her most important obligation in life was to be a mother, not abandon her child throughout the day to gallivant with some boy.

Mother was being unfairly harsh with her assumption. Amber loved Trista as much as any mother would love her child. The guilt of leaving her baby throughout the day ate away at Amber's soul. In all those hours spent with Paulette, she worried and thought so much of her own daughter. How she wished she could have brought Trista with during the day.

Mother would provide the necessary jolt to make this wish a reality. "Amber, I am no longer watching Trista throughout the day. I offered to watch her so you can take classes, not for you to take advantage of me. And we'll see how long this boy stays around when the most important thing in your life is suddenly included in the picture."

The last thing Amber was going to do was inform Mother of her daily activities. Instead, she appeared disappointed and walked off with Trista for some much-needed mother and child time.

On Thursday morning, just like in previous mornings, Amber left her house at 6:30. But this time little Trista sat in the backseat. If all went according to plan, she would accompany Mommy at work.

Today would be another test for Michael. Amber stepped over many obstacles, just to somehow be part of his life. Would Michael do the same and forgive her for being not-so forthcoming?

Amber was an ethereal woman, a dreamer who pursued her many wishes. Often in life she relentlessly pursued those dreams, regardless of any cost or consequence. Any damage or destruction that was caused would surely be corrected. These corrections were often planned out in fantasy.

Amber stood at the front door of the Dickly castle with Trista in one arm and a mommy's necessity bag in the other.

Michael soon answered the door. Needless to say, he was surprised with the presence of the child. "Hi! Who's this?"

Amber broke down in tears. "I'm sorry; I was dishonest with you. She's my daughter. I didn't say anything to you at first."

It was strange talk for Michael, all the apologizing. "Whoa, whoa; what do you mean? This is your daughter?" He quickly pulled the mother and child in the house for it was a cold morning in Sillmac.

"Yes, my mother isn't going to watch her anymore. I don't know what else to do."

Michael smiled at the child, "Well she's pretty."

Cute, little Trista turned and hid her face against Mommy's shoulder; such a bashful child in the sudden presence of a stranger.

Michael continued speaking to Amber, "Well, I don't have a problem with your little one being here. As long as you think you can do both jobs. It'll be nice to have... what did you say her name was?"

"Trista."

"Trista... such a pretty name. Trista would be a welcome addition. The more, the merrier! Paulette ought to really like her!"

As the minutes passed, and Trista was set on the ground to get acclimated to her new environment, Michael began to speak of his and Linsey's reason for having only one child. "We almost lost Paulette, not once, but twice. Linsey miscarried three times before she was pregnant with Paulette. And at one point, it almost looked like Paulette would be the fourth miscarriage. Needless to say, Linsey could no longer take the emotional turmoil of losing babies. After Paulette, we decided not to try for any more. We considered adoption; but after Paulette's accident, Linsey had her hands plenty full."

And so Amber continued to work at the Dickly Castle. She was a regular house wife; getting Paulette ready for the day, making breakfast for what appeared to be her own family and then caring for Trista and Paulette throughout the day.

One might have considered Trista to be an angelic child. She was quiet and not much of a bother. Of course a child at that age certainly has her moments. Trista would sometimes toddle around the family room or grand foyer, and then fall on her bottom or crack her head against the wall. Crying would follow, of course. And there were moments when she grew fussy and cried some. But overall, Trista was a joy to have in the Dickly castle; and something new to put a smile on Paulette's face.

But Amber was getting impatient. When would the moment finally come when she and Michael grew closer together? They shared a destiny; and Amber was to be so much more than a caretaker.

Throughout the days, Michael remained upstairs, behind closed doors in his office. He made phone calls and worked on finances or reports. But there were many hours when non-work related activities were done.

It began by creating what could be considered a death mask of Linsey's statue-head. A thin cloth was placed over Linsey's statue-face so that Plaster of Paris could be applied in the exact same way of creating the original mask.

While doing this, Michael reassured his deceased wife, "Don't worry, Linsey. I'll be extra careful with this… Almost dried, then you can go rest some more."

The second mask would certainly lack the resolution and fine detail of Linsey's original mask. It was only a copy, something to destroy once its purpose had been fulfilled. For you see, Michael could not afford experimenting with Linsey's statue-head while finding the proper flesh-colored paint that would reflect the soft, pink coloring of Linsey's face. When the perfect colors had been found, Michael would finally apply these to Linsey's original statue-head.

The second mask was built up into a full head so that Michael could begin testing various paints. He stood outside on the office balcony, spray painting the copied statue in various places until the perfect blend of sprays produced Linsey's exact coloring.

When the perfect blend had been found, the nerve-racking task of spray painting Linsey's original statue-face underwent. At some point, Michael thought he had ruined his wife's face, forever! The colors weren't blending as well as before, and he nearly broke down in tears. It was pink that needed to be applied first, and then peach. A few layers of spray corrected the original flaw. When fully dried, Linsey's blush was applied. Finally, the work was fully complete; and Michael was satisfied with the result.

* * *

It was a Wednesday afternoon at two o'clock, nearly a week before Thanksgiving. Amber and Paulette sat in the family room, watching trashy talk shows that showcased the lives of trailer park America. Trista lay napping on the loveseat.

Michael carefully descended the staircase and into the foyer while carrying Linsey's statue-head. As he approached the family room, Paulette noticed Father and soon the statue-head in his arms. The statue-head was too real! It was so real, in fact, that it looked as though Father had simply decapitated Mother and carried her head into the family room.

Amber, too, noticed Michael entering the family room with his recently completed piece of art. She recognized it as being Linsey and quickly flipped off the TV. His work of Linsey was very important to Michael. Amber wouldn't allow a trashy talk show to highlight the background of Linsey's presence.

Linsey was placed on the side table next to her photo. A candle was lit, and Michael sat down on the sofa beside Linsey. He softly announced, "Finally, Linsey is complete." He combed his fingers through her hair. "Isn't she beautiful? She's with us, but merely sleeping."

Paulette looked upon the statue-head in horror. It radiated the very color of Mother's beautiful face before she had gotten ill. Father truly lost his mind. Why was he tormenting himself and her with a frightfully realistic head of Mother? It sat on the table, and just as Father said, appeared to be merely sleeping. It looked as though at any moment, Mother would open her eyes and speak.

"It's two o'clock in the afternoon." said Michael. "Linsey would always sit in the family room at this time of day with a cup of tea, just watching the scenery outside. If it was a nice day, she would sit outside on the deck. Amber, do you like tea?"

"Yes, I drink it sometimes." She looked upon the man she loved with compassion. There was something important about this moment, Amber knew it. She offered, "Would you like me to brew us some tea?"

Michael was delighted, "Would you? Oh, during this time of year, Linsey enjoyed a cinnamon stick with her tea. Please be sure to bring one."

Amber left the family room for the kitchen. Ten minutes later, she returned with a tray containing a pot of hot water, four cups, four tea bags and cinnamon stick. She set the tray on the coffee table, and then she looked at Paulette. "I thought maybe you would like a cup of tea as well. We'll let it cool off. Oh, I forgot a straw."

Amber opened all four tea bags, set them in the cups and then poured steamy water over the bags until the cups were filled. Then one cinnamon stick was placed into a cup and handed to Michael.

While Amber did this, Paulette noticed for the first time that Amber's long hair was styled very much like Mother's had been. And it may have been coincidence, but Amber's nurturing, compassionate behavior towards Father was suddenly alarming.

Outside, the cold, autumn air that tossed leaves throughout the yard and gray, overcast skies suggested a day to stay indoors. The candle next to the statue-head provided a warm, peaceful environment along with what was becoming a close-bonded group of people who enjoyed tea.

"Thanksgiving is a week away." said Michael. "Linsey would insist on having Thanksgiving, Christmas and New Years here. It was so easy to fly family out here and put them in hotels so they can join us for the elaborate celebration. We've been invited to join family this Thanksgiving, being that Linsey won't be hosting the celebration. It's so kind and thoughtful of everyone. But I think I want a small celebration this year. Amber, it would mean so much to me if you and Trista would join us for Thanksgiving dinner. Do you have any prior obligations?—family, I'm sure."

"I would love to join you and Paulette for Thanksgiving!" Slowly, but surely, Amber was finding her way into Michael's heart.

Chapter Seven

Throughout the remainder of the week and the few days prior to Thanksgiving, Paulette remained low-key with her new suspicion towards Amber. This was easy, of course, being that spoken words would not express Paulette's mood. Facial expressions could easily be masked, and anything typed on her keyboard was thought out so that no slip of the tongue would reveal something that Paulette kept to herself. She was a teenage girl, like any other, who had her silly fears that were perhaps no worse than that of an ordinary girl.

You and I might see a man and woman who are developing a fondness towards one another and think nothing of it. This is life. But for Paulette, Amber was a strange woman who suddenly swept her way in the home, seduced Father and was beginning to take on subtle appearances of Mother. That in combination of the very, eerie presence of Mother's statue-head, and the way that Amber seemed to encourage Father's adoration of it, had Paulette very uneasy.

Thanksgiving morning was the final straw! Amber must have had an appointment with her hairdresser the previous evening, and had her light-brown hair dyed to auburn. It certainly wasn't strawberry-red like Mother's, but the auburn color did suggest a woman who had long, red hair.

Amber did her usual duties of washing and grooming Paulette once arriving at the Dickly castle. Throughout these moments, Paulette remained somewhat distant towards Amber, making minimal eye contact and wearing a blank expression. Amber assumed that the first holiday without her mother would be very difficult for Paulette.

With Paulette finally dressed and her hair in need of blow-drying, Amber finally spoke words of compassion to the girl. "I know, Honey. This is the first holiday without your mother. It's going to be difficult."

Paulette turned her head to the computer cart, an indication that she wanted it rolled over so she could type a message into the keyboard.

Amber did as asked.

Paulette pecked away at the keyboard with the pencil in her mouth, "What are you doing to my father?"

Amber looked shocked. "Honey, what do you mean?"

"You're doing something to my father. And why does your hair look so much like my mother's?"

Amber sighed, "Paulette, I have always worn my hair like this. I've always had straight, naturally flowing hair. It's just coincidence that your mother wore her hair the same way. If you like, I will bring in photos of myself through the years so you can see."

This answer wasn't good enough for Paulette. "You dyed your hair red."

Amber was quick to respond, "It's auburn, and I always like to have it dyed this color for the holidays. Alright, you know, is that what you're worried about; I'm making moves on your father by trying to remind him of your mother? Let me tell you, I am not your mother. And if your father was attracted to me, I would hope it was because he liked me for who I am."

It was all the proof Paulette needed. Amber admitted it at that very moment. She was hoping that Michael was attracted to her.

Amber sighed, "Honey, I'm sorry. I just realized I am not being empathetic to your situation. I don't know if your father likes me that way. All I know is that he invited Trista and me to celebrate the holiday with you and him. It meant a lot to me. If you don't want me to join you, just let me know. I'll leave once dinner is ready."

Having Amber and Trista join the holiday dinner meant so much to Father. Paulette knew this, and wouldn't dare ask Amber to leave. Aside from that, Paulette didn't mind Amber's presence. She just needed her concerns to be known.

There's a moment in a young person's life when he or she directly approaches an older person with a concern, hoping for resolution or reassurance that a concern isn't true. Shortly after this attempt, it is sometimes learned that nothing comes out of the experience. Words are exchanged, and the younger person is made to feel as though wrongful conclusions had been assumed. And then business goes on as usual. It's a small moment in life when we learn that not everyone is willing to open their hearts truthfully. We learn that most people "dance around an issue".

It was almost as if Amber and Father would have greeted one another in the kitchen with a good morning kiss. They remained some distance from one another but their long-full intention played out in some other world that, although was invisible, was clearly seen between themselves and Paulette.

Amber was so wifely and motherly as she prepared breakfast for the day. She brought with a special blend of pumpkin spice coffee to be brewed. She baked cinnamon rolls, made a huge omelet and sausage patties. She was just as any wife and mother who prepares breakfast on a holiday morning. Lunch would probably be skipped for the day to make room for Thanksgiving feast. It was best that the family eat a hearty breakfast.

At some point, Michael complimented Amber. "You know, I really like your hair. It looks so nice, red."

"Why thank you! I'm glad you like it."

Being that it was Thanksgiving, Michael was sure to take the weekend off from overseeing the business. Throughout the morning and afternoon, he and Amber enjoyed one another's company while cooking those items for Thanksgiving dinner. They laughed together, told brief stories of one another's lives; overall acted like a couple who were falling in love. At some point, Paulette took notice of how happy Father was. Perhaps she was being unfair. Perhaps Amber was the best thing that could have happened to him since Mother died.

And then Amber did the unthinkable. In the heat of the kitchen amidst the smell of turkey, candied yams and pumpkin pie; she set the table for five people. Three place settings were certainly needed for Father, Paulette and Amber. A fourth place setting with a height chair would have been needed for little Trista. Who was the fifth place setting for? Paulette was afraid to find out.

As Father stood, looking out through the family room window, Amber approached and put her hand on his shoulder. "Michael, why don't you have Linsey join us? It's only right."

"Really; would you mind?"

"Of course not. See, I have a place setting for her."

Clearly out of his mind, Father was ecstatic with Amber's offer. "Oh Amber, thank you so much. You don't know how much this means to me." He ran up the flight of stairs and into his bedroom. Moments later, he returned with the realistic statue-head of his late wife, Linsey. "There you go, Linsey. You're still with us, and certainly part of Thanksgiving dinner." He pushed her plate forward, and gently set Linsey down on the table so that her head faced the table as if anyone else who sat down for dinner.

Amber soon brought a candle to the table to be lit and set next to Linsey.

Linsey often felt that Pinot Grigio went well with Thanksgiving turkey. Of course Michael went into the wine cellar for two bottles and returned. "As you like; Pinot Grigio!" Michael poured a glass for Linsey in addition to three others for himself, Amber and Paulette.

And so as Paulette was wheeled to the table, it was necessary to take sight of the most disturbingly real replica of Mother, who faced everyone at the table. She looked to be merely sleeping with her eyes that could have opened at any second.

Father led the blessing. "It's been a very, sad couple of years for us; the saddest being the recent loss of Linsey…" Father looked at Paulette, "… your mother. But I believe we have much to be thankful for this holiday. All of us are in good health, Paulette has a friend who can take care of her throughout the day; and it feels as though we have new members of the family—Amber and little Trista. Despite our unfortunate loss, we still have much to be thankful for this year!"

Although this was a special holiday dinner along with what was turning into a warm, fuzzy day between her and Michael; Amber hadn't put the duty aside of feeding Paulette first. Mouthfuls of turkey, cranberries and stuffing were nearly forced into Paulette's mouth; all the while the frightening replica of Mother watched intently from across the table. For so many years the family had visited church every Sunday. But there was a new god in the house, a twisted idol of the woman who had given birth and raised Paulette until her life's end. The new priestess in the house attempted to be an incarnation of the woman this idol represented. With the appearance of the statue's eyes being closed, the occasional change of lighting that was brought on by dance of the candle flames sometimes made it appear as though Mother had no eyes. During these eerie seconds, Paulette's brain would fill the gap with some missing expression that she assumed Mother would have at the moment.

The thing glared from across the table, "Eat your Thanksgiving dinner, Paulette! That's it; eat every bite of it! Trust the priestess who leads the family into my worship!"

Even Mother had gone mad.

* * *

In recent times, a portable crib had been placed in the guest room upstairs. This was used for those moments when little Trista needed some downtime or a nap. For Thanksgiving night, she and Mommy would sleep in the guest room of the Dickly castle, as Mommy was eager for more warm and friendly conversation with Michael.

Paulette was in bed for the evening, and Trista slept soundly in her crib. Downstairs in the quiet, candlelit family room; Amber enjoyed the company of Michael and his wife, Linsey. Amber was such a joy to have around. She brought such cheer to the Dickly castle.

Michael suggested, "You don't have to worry about driving home tonight. What do you say I go down in the cellar and get another bottle of wine?"

"Sure…" said Amber.

Michael left her alone with Linsey, whose face perpetually changed expressions under the flicker of candlelight. Amber didn't mind. The statue was important to Michael. The more she seemed to share his adoration, the closer Michael became to Amber.

He returned with a bottle of Linsey's Pinot Noir and three wine glasses. Once the bottle was open, a nearly full glass was poured for Linsey. Amber was given the second glass; Michael took the third. Upon taking the first sip, he immediately spoke of where the case of Pinot Noir had been purchased from. "It was our last family trip together. I think that was my last time seeing Linsey in good health. She became sick shortly upon returning home."

Amber had an interesting game she liked to play in which she would think to herself of where she might have been while hearing someone's story of the past. She certainly wasn't going to probe of the exact day of the family trip, or of the moment when Linsey became ill. But from what Amber could gather, Linsey grew ill around the time that Trista's father had left her— possibly around the time when Amber set her heart on finding an older man who needed her. It always amazed Amber of how connected people were. Oh, but she wouldn't mention her shared, cosmic connection to Michael. He might not have understood the ethereal world where Amber resided.

As the wine in their glasses neared half empty, Michael was suddenly easy with placing his arm on the top of the sofa cushion where Amber sat. Being in this position, he began to softly comb his fingers through her long, auburn hair.

Amber asked, "So where did you and Linsey first meet?"

"At a party when I was in my early twenties. My buddy encouraged me to go, but I wanted to stay home. My girlfriend at the time had broken up with me. I wasn't in the mood to go out. Had I not allowed my buddy to convince me, I probably would have never met my future wife."

Had the room not been dimly-lit, Michael would have seen Amber suddenly blush while she said, "Well your girlfriend at the time wasn't too smart. I would have never broken up with you."

At that, Michael's face drew near to Amber's. Then he kissed her. The kisses gave her goose bumps and butterflies that took off in every direction. Soon, Michael took her glass and set it on the coffee table next to his. More kisses were given, this time building in intensity. Before you know it, the two lay on the sofa, making out for quite some time. How long do those who fall in love make out for the first time? Love doesn't understand time. Hours might feel like minutes as both desire more and more kisses.

With her long, auburn-dyed hair; the young woman who lay beside and face-to-face with Michael was nearly Linsey in the flesh. How Michael remembered and missed his Linsey of decades ago. In those days, the sadness in their lives was so far away. The young lovers were so carefree, only living according to the time dictated by love. Every deep and passionate kiss exchanged with Amber returned Michael to those days with Linsey. Amber was wonderful and someone who Michael needed more of.

Sometimes he would pull away for brief glance of the young woman. It was Linsey! Her face and expressions of love were the same.

Amber smiled, "What's happening with us? Where are we going with this relationship?"

As Michael recalled, Linsey had asked similar things upon their first time of making out.

Chapter Eight

Waking up later than usual, Amber slept in the guest bedroom of the Dickly castle. It was Black Friday, and an overflow of duties was suddenly apparent to Amber. Little Trista jumped up and down in the portable crib, expecting to have the previous night's diaper changed and to have a bonding moment with Mommy while she lay on her lap, drinking a bottle. In addition to this, Paulette was surely awake in her room and expecting to start the day. It was nearly eight o'clock in the morning. Every other morning, Amber was sure to be there by seven o'clock. Hopefully Paulette would understand.

After a quick change of Trista's diaper, Amber walked into Paulette's bedroom with Trista toddling behind. Paulette was not happy! She wore a bitter frown that asked, "Where have you been?" Like most people, Paulette needed to use the bathroom. Having to wait was unnecessary torture.

Amber was apologetic, "Oh, I'm so sorry, Honey. Let me get you into the bathroom!"

But there was further reason for Paulette's outrage as Amber wore a pair of Mother's pajamas! How dare she stay the night to be up late with Father, then to wear Mother's pajamas? If Paulette had been able to mobilize herself, she would have surely clawed Amber to shreds. The deepening bitterness on her face provided this realization to Amber.

Amber was in no mood for the teenage girl's attitude. Trista began to whine for her bottle, and Paulette needed to be cleaned and groomed for the day. In addition, breakfast was to be made. It was a busy morning, indeed.

This was a morning when Trista would have to lay on Paulette's bed, propped up on a pillow to drink a bottle. Mommy needed to care for Paulette.

As for Amber, the fantasies of hauling off and striking Paulette with a sharp smack to her face played a couple times in her mind. Perhaps it wouldn't have been such a bad idea to fill the tub with more water than usual, and let Paulette slip under for a couple seconds. Maybe that would have cooled things down.

Instead, Amber kept her cool and handled Paulette the way a grown woman should. Amber knew what the problem was. She wore Linsey's pajamas that covered her own naked breasts. She spent the night and experienced some romance with the man she loved, who just so happened to be Paulette's father. Tired of being criticized for her hair and for seducing the man she loved, Amber voiced her confrontation in one simple phrase. "So what's up?"

Paulette returned a pouty look.

"You've been giving me attitude since I came in your room this morning. I said I was sorry for being late. I know it had to be uncomfortable to wait for the bathroom, and I feel bad. So are you going to dwell on this for the rest of the day?"

Amber could feel Paulette's need to lunge from the bathtub and tear her to shreds. It was time to nip this in the bud. In no way could Paulette destroy the romance that had finally ignited between Amber and Michael. Amber would speak with the girl's father, alone.

Once the pouty and very, bitter Paulette had been dressed and her hair blow-dried; Amber carried her own daughter out of the room and shut the door behind. Michael was already up, as evidenced by the smell of coffee that brewed in the kitchen.

She lightly bounced down the stairs with Trista in her arm and then turned towards the kitchen. Amber greeted her lover, "Good morning!"

"Hey, good morning! Where's Paulette?"

Now don't think for one second that Amber would have made up a wicked lie about Paulette. She hated lying, and there was no reason to do so. In her world, Amber truly felt that something important needed to be mentioned to Michael. Amber met Michaels query with a serious look, indicating a problem. "Well, I thought I should call this to your attention. Obviously, Paulette is aware that I spent the night here and doesn't like it."

Michael was surprised, "What?"

"Michael, if looks could kill! I think she has some jealousy, which I totally understand. Yesterday she asked me if I was hitting on you and stuff. She knows what's happening between us, Michael. I don't want to get between you and your daughter…"

Michael quickly interrupted, "Hey, hey; she's not going to get between us. Some things have obviously changed between you and me and it's time I have a talk with Paulette. Could you take the rest of the day off? I'm going to have some alone time with her."

Alone time? That could go in either direction. Amber had no choice but to agree, "Sure…"

Michael smiled, "Don't worry; you'll get holiday pay, and maybe a little bonus."

* * *

It's important to understand that back at home, Amber's mother and father were clueless of their daughter's activities. They had no idea that she was spending time with the wealthiest man in Sillmac—probably the wealthiest man in the entire state. They had no idea that the owner of the ever-expanding Dickly's hardware was in love with their daughter. Furthermore, Mother and Father had no idea of Amber's whereabouts for over twenty-four hours.

As soon as the opened door produced Amber's presence with Trista in her arms, Mother immediately jumped up. "Where the hell have you been?"

"Sorry, I spent the night at my boyfriend's."

Mother nearly shrieked out of rage, "Without calling us? Without letting us know where you were? And you missed Thanksgiving dinner with all your relatives? We thought something was wrong! And you have Trista with you? Amber, what the hell is wrong with you?"

Amber remained calm, "Sorry, Mom; I should have called."

Father entered the room. For him, it was the day after Thanksgiving, a floating holiday provided by the company. But he had been equally as worried as Mother. "Where have you been young lady?"

"At my boyfriend's; I spent the night."

"Spent the night? With your kid there?" He looked at Mother, shook his head and then exhaled his pent-up frustration before continuing. "Alright, that's enough of this crap! Things are going to change around here! I don't like what I'm seeing!" He turned back towards Mother, "You want to tell her about the new rules here at home?"

Amber was certainly an adult, and too old to be grounded. But just like many young adults in their early twenties who live at home while appearing unemployed or not in school, it was necessary to dictate guidelines. It was time to lay down some rules for the irresponsible, young woman who appeared to do nothing more than come and go as she pleased while making babies.

Mother announced her unorganized list of rules that she and Father created while discussing the recent observations of their twenty-two-year-old daughter. "As long as you are living in this house and raising my granddaughter, you will not run around with some boy all day long and come home when you please.

You will get a job and pay us rent. If you want to seriously consider going to school, we can talk about that.

As far as staying out all night with Trista, you now have a curfew. We want you home right after work; none of this business of staying out until ten o'clock the next morning!

And you will tell us *exactly* where you are going! It's time you act like a responsible adult and mother."

Father interrupted. "Can I just ask where you are for ten hours a day with your kid?"

Amber sighed and finally let the truth known, "I'm working, Dad."

This didn't make sense to Father. "Working… with Trista?" It must have been another lie.

"Yes, Dad; I take care of a paralyzed girl throughout the day."

This story was becoming more interesting by the second. "Since when?"

"It's Michael Dickly, Dad. He hired me to take care of his daughter after his wife died."

"Michael Dickly, president of Dickly's Hardware store?"

"Yes…"

Like a cat just seconds from pouncing its prey, Mother approached Amber in disbelief, "How did you get involved in that?"

"I went to her funeral and met Michael. And remember the day I made braciole for a friend? I made it for Michael and brought it to his house and had dinner with him. He asked if I wanted to take care of his daughter."

One could have nearly seen the steam pouring out of Mother's head at that moment. "You went to that woman's funeral and met her husband?"

Father asked, "Well how much is he paying you to do that?"

"A thousand dollars a week..."

This new knowledge of Amber's mysterious activities and whereabouts put a whole, new spin on things. Amber wasn't an irresponsible, young woman who appeared to do nothing more than come and go as she pleased while making babies. She was something else in Mother's eyes.

Mother hauled off and smacked her child across the face. "You're nothing but a gold-digging tramp! You wait for a rich man's wife to die, and then introduce yourself at the funeral! You invite yourself into his home, pretending to offer a home-cooked meal! You seduce him and spend the night at his house on Thanksgiving! And now you're taking his money?" Another sharp slap was given across Amber's face "I'll see to it that Mr. Dickly gets his money back, and apologize for my daughter's trampy behavior! And don't you dare go back there!"

The wrongful accusations, painful slaps to the cheek and the frustration of being treated like a child brought Amber to tears. "Mom, you can't do that!"

"I'll do whatever I damn well please as long as you live under my roof!"

* * *

It was now the evening of Black Friday. Retail stores closed their doors and battered shoppers returned home with nearly maxed out credit cards. As for Amber, she sat on her bed while little Trista slept soundly in her crib. It had been nearly forty-eight hours of intense emotions for Amber. Much time was spent with Michael, falling in love on Thanksgiving. She woke up nearly hung over Friday morning from the previous day's excessive eating, excessive wine and late night passion. Paulette could have murdered her with the belief that Father had been seduced. And then Amber had to be slapped and accused of horrible things that just weren't true.

Poor Amber: nearly in tears from a surge of conflicting emotions. It wasn't Amber's fault that Michael was wealthy. She only wished for a man that needed her love in a dark moment. If this man earned a modest salary, Amber would have loved him just the same. For you see, Amber existed in a different world where material things were of little importance. Only true love mattered to Amber. Was this not what Mother taught her early in life?

Where was her true love? Only Michael could have taken the sadness away at that moment. Amber needed to hear his voice; hear that the wrongful accusations of Mother were not true. He was her prince that could have rescued and saved her from this low state. But why hadn't he called? It was nine o'clock in the evening. Did he have second thoughts of Amber? Did Paulette make up some wicked lie? Or maybe Michael decided it was best to cool it with Amber for the sake of his daughter?

Such was the regular misfortune in Amber's life. It was why she remained a dreamer. Sometimes Amber truly felt that she had only her fantasies to live on. As she sat on the bed with her knees pulled to her chest while gazing through the window at the starry sky, teardrops rolled from her cheeks and onto her knee. How could he abandon her this way? What right did he have to play with her heart, build up her hopes and then leave her alone at such a dark moment? Amber was there for Michael in his darkest moment, befriending his daughter and filling the home with a loving presence. And what did she have for it in return? She was sent home to Mother for a slap to the face and to be called a tramp.

Well Amber was too good to be treated this way! She deserved every bit of truth at that moment and decided to call Michael's home. She had his number from the phonebook, found on the day after Linsey's funeral when Amber visited the Dickly castle with braciole.

Only two callout rings were necessary to produce the sound of Michael's voice, "Hello?"

Amber's lips quivered as her eyes flooded with tears. "Michael?"

"Yeah, hi!"

"How come you haven't called me?"

There was a brief pause, "Well, you never gave me your number, silly. You're not listed in the phonebook, either. I've been waiting for you to call!" Before you think it was a lie of Michael's, keep in mind that this was 1994. The phonebook was pretty much the only immediate source of looking for a person. The internet was a challenging thing to maneuver, if you happened to be one of only ten million people familiar with it. Google was two years into the future, and nearly a decade to develop into what it is today.

How silly of Amber! Of course! She had simply gone to his house every Monday through Friday. There was never a reason to call Michael or for him to call her. Up until yesterday, she was only an employee who reported to work.

"Oh, I'm sorry!" Now Amber was nearly embarrassed with a possible display of immature behavior. Did she sound like a little girl in that moment?

"That's okay; it was just a silly misunderstanding. I've been waiting to hear from you all day. I had a nice, long, heart-to-heart talk with Paulette. She understands everything, and she's sorry for how she acted."

It was such an emotional day for Amber. Floods of tears came from her eyes as she found it necessary to lift the microphone end of the handset away from her mouth. She couldn't let sniffles be heard on Michael's end. Everything was fine between her, Michael and Paulette. Mother was wrong; people truly loved and had respect for Amber. How glad she was to have called Michael!

"Are you crying?" The nasal voice was impossible to disguise.

"Yes, I'm sorry. My mom and dad kind of yelled at me when I came home. I should have called yesterday to tell them I was spending the night."

"Uh oh; they're mad that you spent the night at my place?"

"Yes…" More tears streamed down her cheeks. "They don't want me to see you anymore."

"No! I need you! I was going to wait until the next time I see you, but I need to make some business trips in the upcoming weeks. I need you to stay here and take care of Paulette while I'm gone."

Stay at the Dickly castle? Act as the woman in charge while her man was gone on business? It was the next best thing to being Michael Dickly's wife! Amber certainly couldn't turn down such an offer!

Chapter Nine

Not a day could be wasted! Living at the Dickly castle would begin the Saturday after Black Friday. Michael would leave for his first trip on the first of December. In 1994, that would have come on the following Thursday. Amber needed to quickly be situated and set up for a more permanent residence at the Dickly castle. Aside from that, Amber was no longer simply Paulette's caretaker who visited Monday through Friday. Amber was Michael's lover, and there was no reason to spend weekends apart.

And there was no need to obey over-controlling Mother! Amber walked out the door on Saturday morning with Trista in her arms while Mother and Father slept. She would call later in the week to patch things up with Mother; but for now, Amber had her own family to take care of.

Amber was a very, intelligent, young woman. She knew that Michael had an underlying cause for trusting her to care for Paulette while he traveled. Michael was in love with Amber, and wished to test her ability to be alone with Paulette. In fact, this test was probably mentioned by Michael during his father and daughter talk. Paulette would report any wrongdoings or mistreating to Father. But Amber didn't worry about that. As she planned, Amber and Paulette would have so much fun together in those weeks alone. Amber would be Paulette's best friend; her older sister; even her adopted mother.

Michael opened the front door before Amber knocked. "Good morning!"

"Good morning!"

"We'll get you a key; no need to knock anymore."

A couple sweet kisses were exchanged once Amber and Trista had been let in. And after Trista was set on the floor to toddle and explore her environment, Michael embraced Amber for some deeper, loving kisses. He briefly pulled away, "I wouldn't blow you off. Is that what you thought last night?"

Amber shrugged her shoulders.

Michael noticed a barely-noticeable red mark near Amber's left eye. "What happened? Is that a welt or something?"

"Yeah, my mom slapped me."

"She slapped you? That's child abuse." Then he smiled and kissed Amber some more. "I'm glad you're staying here. It means a lot to me."

Although in love with Amber, Michael wasn't ready to have her sleep in his bed with him. For one, Linsey slept with Michael each night. There were pictures of Linsey on both sides of the bed. And Michael enjoyed his moments in the evening when he and Linsey talked about the business, Paulette and other family matters. Amber assumed that this was the reason and had no problem agreeing to sleep in the guest bedroom. But she also assumed that through time, the guest bedroom would become Trista's bedroom as Mommy would eventually sleep with the man whose name would become Daddy.

But before anything else was dreamed or imagined, Amber had some serious business that needed attention. It was five minutes after seven o'clock in the morning. Paulette was surely awake for the day.

Alone, Amber entered Paulette's room and carefully greeted the girl who would surely become her adopted daughter. "Hi…"

Paulette only looked at Amber as she approached her bed. When near, Amber bent over and hugged her. "I'm so sorry;

I'm so sorry about yesterday." She pulled away and continued to lightly comb her fingers through Paulette's hair. "I told you there would be challenges. Yesterday was just one of them. I want you to know that I will take very, good care of you and your father. I won't do anything to harm you, okay?"

Paulette remained expressionless—forgiveness; trust; maybe fear?

While washing Paulette in the tub, Amber spoke of the planned activities during those weeks when Michael was away on business. "I'm going to have your father show me how to use the chairlift for the van. We'll get out of here throughout the week, do some shopping and have lunch. The holidays are here. Downtown Sillmac is totally lit up with the Christmas tree in the center of town. We'll have a lot of fun; just you, me and Trista."

That Saturday was 180 degrees from the previous day. Treated like a child only twenty-four hours ago, Amber was now the woman of the Dickly castle who prepared breakfast for her family. And there was no reason to disguise the feelings towards her man. Michael had no problem giving a friendly kiss to Amber as he entered the kitchen. They all sat down and had their breakfast. And of course, Paulette was fed before Amber ate. Such is one of the many sacrifices of a loving mother.

Amber maintained the practice of preparing tea at 1:45 in the afternoon. For as she, Paulette and Trista lounged in the family room some time after lunch; Linsey would come downstairs with Michael for afternoon tea. It was during this Saturday teatime, the day after Black Friday, when Amber announced to Michael that she would like to take Paulette on afternoon outings while Michael was gone away on business.

The candlelight flickered along Linsey's face as she appeared a bit concerned with Amber's suggestion. Could Amber really handle the paralyzed girl out in public?

Michael noticed his wife's concern, "Linsey my dear, I think Amber is capable of taking Paulette on outings." Then he turned his attention back to Amber. "I'll have to show you how to use the chairlift on the van. And that's totally easy; just lower it and wheel Paulette in. Securing her is the important thing. What do you think, Paulette? Would you like that?"

Paulette eagerly nodded in agreement.

* * *

Hopefully there would be many cuddly evenings with Michael after Paulette and Trista had gone to bed. The two sat beside one another under the soft glow of dimmed family room light. In the distance, Linsey flickered as she sat on one of the side tables.

Michael suggested, "Well, we don't have to polish off a bottle of wine every night. But it's Saturday night. Why don't I pull a bottle of Pinot Noir from the cellar and we can all share a glass?"

How could Amber turn down his suggestion? "Sure…"

While Michael paid a visit to the wine cellar, Amber occasionally glanced at Linsey. Would she always be there in the background of Amber's life? Would Linsey always share the bottle of wine between her and Michael? Three was such an awkward number as there are four glasses in a bottle, perfect for lovers to enjoy just the right amount of two glasses on a romantic evening like this. How long would Amber have to adore the statue-head of a woman that was deceased?

As usual, the first glass was poured for Linsey and set beside her. The second was poured for Amber, and the third was poured for Michael.

After taking a couple sips of wine, Michael announced, "Well Amber, I was thinking of having Linsey watch over you and girls while I'm gone. I'll leave her out here on the table. But please light a candle for her and offer a cup of tea at two o'clock each day."

Great, just want Amber wanted! But adoring Linsey meant so much to Michael. "Oh, I'd love to have Linsey watch over us. And I'll be sure to enjoy tea with her every afternoon at two o'clock."

Chapter Ten

It was the morning of December 1st, exactly one week from Thanksgiving. Michael's baggage sat at the front door, and the family shared breakfast while waiting for the limousine to arrive. Michael wasn't going to drive to the airport or bother Amber to take him. A successful man like Michael travels in style. He flew first class, stayed at luxury penthouse hotels and arranged for limousines to transport him while not flying. What else would you expect from the founder and owner of Dickly's Hardware?

Michael took a sip from his coffee before speaking. "Hey, Christmas is just around the corner. There's a large storage closet at the other end of the house that has the Christmas tree, decorations and stuff. If you feel up to it, why don't you decorate the house for Christmas? I'd love to see the place lit up when I get back."

It sounded like an excellent idea to Amber. "Sure! It'll definitely feel like Christmas when you get back."

After breakfast, Michael invited Amber into his office upstairs. It was the first time she had ever stepped foot in the impressive room with oversized desk, comfy executive chair, sofas against the walls and a dry bar next a library of business and success books.

"I'm going to give you this." Michael presented a check to Amber. "Not only is it your entire month's worth of salary, but some additional money for living expenses and things." It was a check for ten thousand dollars! "I'm trusting you with that. Please take excellent care of Paulette. I know you will."

Amber immediately embraced Michael. "Oh Michael, you know I'll take care of her. And I appreciate everything that you've done for me and the way that you trust me."

The two kissed for some moments, realizing that it would be a week before seeing one another, again. And then the doorbell rang.

"That's my ride!" Michael dashed out of the office door and down the stairs to open the front door.

A limousine driver greeted Michael, "Good morning, Sir. I'm here to take you to the airport."

"Excellent! Can you load my baggage while I say goodbye to everyone?"

"Certainly, Sir!"

Michael kissed and hugged his daughter. It was the first time Father would travel since Mother died. "I'll be home in about a week. You okay with Amber?"

Paulette nodded, yes.

More kisses were given to Amber, followed by hugs and a kiss to Trista's cheek. Then Michael walked out the door and to the limousine. He waved goodbye before stepping in. Finally, the musical horn tooted as the large, white limousine drove out of the horseshoe driveway and descended the small mountain.

Amber was now alone with her daughter and Paulette. She was the woman of the Dickly castle who was entrusted to care for the home. Her role was a far cry from what Mother accused her of nearly a week ago. But on that morning of December 1st, Amber would learn as to just how powerful a mother can be. A mother can step in her daughter's life at any time and decide what is right or what should happen. Don't think for one second that eighteen or twenty-one is a magical number that guarantees freedom and independence from over-controlling parents who cannot let go.

It was not more than an hour after Michael left. Amber browsed the enormous Christmas closet that could have easily qualified as a workshop. A huge, towering tree was positioned on a stand with wheels and already decorated with lights and ornaments. At least she didn't have to worry about setting up the tree! Amber only needed to wheel it out to the family room. Countless decorations that could never be put up in one season were stacked and lined up on shelves. And then there were bins of outdoor decorations; statues of Santa Clause, illuminated arctic and forest creatures along with a nativity scene that could easily have been used at a cathedral. The Dickly family went all out for Christmas! Little did Amber know that there were additional workshop-sized closets for Easter and Halloween! Yes, the Dickly castle was HUGE!

Suddenly, the doorbell rang. Who could it have been? Amber scurried across the marble-tiled floor to the grand foyer. Opening the door yielded the ugly site of seething Mother who was seconds from slapping Amber.

Amber wasn't scared. This was her house and her life, now. "Well hi, Mom. I see you found Michael's house. Come-on in!"

Stepping aside to let the woman in, it almost felt as though Mother believed she was fearsome. She was such a delusional woman!

Once inside, Mother whispered harshly, "Get Trista and get your coat! It's time to come home. And where's Mr. Dickly?"

"Michael's out of town, Mom. I'm taking care of his house and his daughter."

One could nearly see the steam pouring out of Mother's face. "You had no business leaving without telling us where you were going! And I told you not to come here anymore! What are the new rules? Do you remember the new rules?"

"Mom, in case you haven't realized, I moved out. I'm living here now. Michael is my boyfriend and I'm taking care of his daughter."

Mother didn't care about that. "Well does he have family who could take care of her?"

"No Mom, they all live out of state!"

"Well how long would it take for someone to get here?"

Amber sighed, "I'm watching his daughter, Mom! I'm not just going to leave her alone with someone else." Amber noticed Paulette watching from the other side of the family room. She felt it best to introduce her to Mother. "Why don't you come into the family room and meet Paulette?"

Mother followed her daughter and then stopped in front of Paulette's wheelchair. Her mood changed to being friendly to disguise her delusional and psychotic personality. "Hi, is Amber really taking care of you while your father is gone?"

Paulette nodded.

"You actually trust her? I'm her mother."

Paulette maintained a blank expression.

Amber informed Mother, "She can't talk, Mom. She had a head injury as a little girl and lost the ability to speak. Plus, she's paralyzed from the neck, down."

Mother sighed and looked at the floor in a brief second of contemplation. Then she looked up at her granddaughter who stood next to Mommy. "Alright Trista, come with me. We're going home." Trista was one aspect in Amber's life that Mother could control.

Amber immediately scooped up Trista. "I don't think so! You're not taking her anywhere."

Although her blood boiled, Mother remained calm. "Amber, give me Trista. I'm taking her home. You are not responsible enough to take care of her. Plus I'm not leaving my granddaughter in an environment like this."

Amber nearly exploded. "Like what, Mom? What's so wrong with this? Is it because I've moved out and you can't control me anymore?"

"*Give… me… Trista*! I'm not going to tell you again!" Seeing that her daughter had no intention of surrendering the child, she aggressively approached with her arms out, ready to snatch Trista from Amber's arms.

But Amber quickly retreated, turned around and ran for the stairs with Trista in her arms. As if she had wings, Amber soared to the second level and into the guest bedroom where Trista was safely placed in the portable crib. She dashed out of the room and shut the door behind her. By the time she reached the stairs, Mother could be seen on the lower level with her foot on the first step.

Like a tigress that protected its offspring, Amber screamed down to her mother, "Don't you dare come up here! Don't you dare come up those stairs!"

Mother remained calm while making a slow and careful ascent. "Amber, I am taking Trista home with me. It's for the best."

Amber screamed in return, "I'm calling the police!"

Mother yelled back, "Fine, call the police! You'll see that they take my side once they arrive."

Mother was crazy! Did she really believe that she was in the right? As the woman of the house who now found it necessary to protect her home and children, Amber ran into Michael's office and dialed 911. "Yes, my Mother is at my house and trying to take my daughter from me!"

Of course it was a strange call for a police dispatcher in Sillmac to receive. Did the grandmother have custody of the caller's child? And once given the address of the Dickly castle, the call was all the more peculiar.

It's interesting to consider Mother's actions in that very moment while Amber called the police. She certainly could have run to the bedroom and snatched up Trista while Amber talked on the phone. Perhaps she was fearful that any screaming and fighting would have been recorded by the dispatcher.

But in the moments of waiting for police to arrive, Amber had all she could do keep Mother from passing her on the stairway. Mother appeared convinced that she had every right to take Trista, and stood at the middle of the stairway. Trista cried and cried in her crib. It was too early for a nap, and there was no reason to be abandoned in the closed room.

Mother continuously announced, "I'm coming up, Amber."

"No you won't! The police are on their way!"

Finally, the doorbell rang. Amber ran down the stairs and past her mother to answer it. But wouldn't you know it? Mother went right up the stairs and into the guest room to save crying Trista.

Amber was a frantic mess while letting the police officer in. "It's my mother! She's trying to take my daughter!"

The police officer took sight of the calm, gentle grandmother who slowly descended the stairs while comforting a child who was in tears. "There, there; Grandma has you. It's not right that Mommy locks you in the room like that."

Then Mother greeted the police officer. "Well hello; I suppose my daughter called you out; probably didn't tell you how she puts my granddaughter in danger. Look, she's locked in her room to cry. My daughter is not responsible, and I wish to take this little one home with me."

The officer shook his head in disbelief, "Folks, I don't have time to settle stupid, domestic disputes." Unfortunately for the officer, he did have to investigate the call and make a report. He looked over to Amber's mother who was now on the main level. "Ma'am, do you want to come outside and answer a few questions so we can get to the bottom of this?"

Amber immediately noticed that the police officer was older, and was possibly able to relate to Mother, more-so than her.

Would Amber be discriminated against in this moment because of her young age?

Mother answered the police officer, "Certainly, I'd be happy to. Seeing that my granddaughter is finally calm, I would expect to bring her with."

The officer didn't care at that moment. "That's fine; it'll only be a minute."

Amber watched in maddening disbelief as Mother walked out of the house with Trista in her arms! Then Mother sat in the police car while speaking to the officer. This was unreal! What on Earth was there to talk about? Amber called the police to have Mother removed from the premises in a means to protect her own daughter. Instead, Mother now sat in a police car with Trista in her arms! There was no way that a child could be taken away just out of words and accusations alone!

Amber paced the floors, nearing lifting her hands to punch the air in frustration. Every second was painful, knowing that Trista was in a police car and surrounded by discussions of how bad Mommy was. But Amber did nothing wrong! Instead, Mother was crazy! It's not a crime to grow up and move out of the house. By next year Amber could be married to Michael. Amber was a functional, contributing adult to society.

Five minutes later Mother, Trista and the officer emerged from the police car. The three walked into the Dickly castle, and then the officer spoke to Amber. "Alright, your mom seems to have your little one under control. Wanna step outside and have a little chat for a few?"

Amber glared at her mother while passing by.

Mother snapped back, "Don't you look at me like that young lady! You did this all to yourself!"

Once outside, the officer shut the door of the Dickly castle behind him and put a firm grasp on Amber's shoulder. "Alright, cool it! Show some respect to your mother, huh? Let's go in the car and talk."

While Amber sat in the back of the police car, Mother stood in the Dickly castle with little Trista in her arms. How did this happen? How did Amber lose control?

The officer asked, "Alright, the one thing I'm curious about: who are you? I mean why are you at Mr. Dickly's house? Where is Mr. Dickly; is he here?"

Amber loudly and clearly answered with the only truth there was, "I'm Michael's girlfriend and I live here. Michael is away on a business trip and I'm taking care of his daughter."

But at that moment, Amber was guilty until proven innocent. "Oh, so you're Mr. Dickly's girlfriend? Right; so Mr. Dickly lost his wife a couple months ago, now you're living here as his girlfriend and taking care of his kid?"

Amber nodded her head, yes.

"See, I have a problem with that. Your driver's license does not list this as your residence..."

Amber quickly interrupted, "I just moved in last week!"

The officer was outraged, "Excuse me; I'm talking! Please don't interrupt me when I'm talking, alright? You wanna see your baby go home with your mom? I can do that!"

Amber's eyes roared with flames at the officer's threat.

The officer continued, "So I'm going to talk to Mr. Dickly's daughter and find out exactly who you are, so you better not be lying to me!" The officer lit up a cigarette before continuing. "So let's talk about you. Your mom seems to think that you are irresponsible and that you put your little one in dangerous situations. She says that you are gone for over ten hours a day, running around with guys and stuff. I guess you sometimes leave for over twenty-four hours. You think that's good for your kid?"

Amber calmly replied, "We're here at Michael's house. I've told my mother that plenty of times. And I moved in with him on Saturday."

The officer exhaled cigarette smoke, "So you want me to be-lieve that your mom is making up all these lies about you, just to control your life and take your daughter away from you?"

Amber remained silent.

"Look, why don't you just let your mom take your kid home. She obviously has some concern and feels you can't take care of your daughter. I guess you leave your kid locked up in a room to cry? Let Grandma take care of her."

Amber shook her head, "I'm not letting anyone take my baby. And my mother has totally exaggerated everything to you."

The officer was persistent. "Come-on, just give your mom the baby."

"No! She will not have her. I love my daughter and she lives here with me!"

Frustrated, the officer opened his door, walked around the vehicle and let Amber out. "I still want to talk to Mr. Dickly's daughter and get her side of the story."

Inside the house; Amber and her mother (who still had Trista in her arms) were ordered to wait in kitchen out of Paulette's view. The officer could be heard walking into the family room and greeting the paralyzed girl.

"I just want to ask you a few questions. First of all, I'm sorry about all the commotion today. Is your father out of town…? Is Amber here to take care of you while he's gone…? Are you unable to talk; that's why you only nod…? Okay, I'll just ask simple questions and you nod yes or no.

Amber says that she is your father's girlfriend and that she lives here. Is that true…? Does she treat you right…? Does she treat her baby alright…? You don't see her hitting the baby or leaving her in the room to cry…? She doesn't leave the diaper unchanged for hours and hours…? She feeds her baby…? Do you ever see Amber bring other men in the house while your father is gone…? Do you think I should let Amber have her baby...? You think she's responsible enough...? Should I give Amber's mother the baby...?"

A police officer who played judge, jury and executioner: who the hell did this guy think he was? Did the officer really believe that he had the authority to conduct an investigation and give sole custody of a child to a grandmother? You would be surprised of the power that police officers have in rural, isolated areas. And even if he had no authority to operate in such a manner, imagine the time lost and frustration endured while Amber legally battled for returned custody of her own daughter.

The police officer entered the kitchen and spoke to Amber's mother. "Alright, legally your daughter hasn't broken any laws. She's of legal age, and according to Mr. Dickly's daughter, she lives here." The officer turned to Amber with a harsh voice, "And get your driver's license updated, you understand?"

Amber nodded.

The officer turned back to Mother, "I'm sorry, I'm afraid I have no choice but to let your daughter have her baby."

Mother was outraged, "What? You've got to be kidding mc!"

"I'm sorry. Go ahead; give the baby back to your daughter."

In a most bizarre moment, little Trista began to cry as Amber pulled her baby out of Grandma's arms. This was terribly embarrassing! Why was Trista doing this?

Grandma immediately pointed out, "Why, she doesn't want her mother. She doesn't want to be left alone here with her. Can't you see that?"

The officer replied, "Ma'am, there's nothing I can do about it. That's her daughter and she's of legal age. Let's go, time to leave."

"But..."

"Let's go...! *Let's go...!*" It was necessary for the officer to physically remove Mother from the Dickly castle and escort the woman to her car. The officer followed Mother out of the horse-shoe driveway and down the mountainous, spiraling driveway to ensure that she left the premises and made her way back onto the highway.

Now alone with Trista crying in her arms, Amber gazed out the front window at the cold, gray, overcast, outside world. It was winter in Sillmac with dangerous temperatures; roads that could suddenly ice before salt trucks arrived.

Mother was such an evil woman! How Amber hated lying, especially when crafted to manipulate people's lives. Mother had been an expert of doing this as long as Amber could remember. Why were such wicked people permitted to act out their harmful deeds without consequence? And how many more times would Amber need to suffer at the hands of her over-controlling mother?

If only there was a way for Mother to finally be punished for her years of mental abuse and her inability to allow Amber to live her own life.

Trista continued cry out for Grandma.

"Trista, baby, what's wrong with you?" This was very, un-usual behavior from the child. She and Amber had a close bond, and Trista was always happy and cheerful while in the Dickly castle. "Trista, that's enough. Grandma just went home. You'll see her again."

But Trista only cried all the louder. Amber had no choice but to give the child some time out in her crib. As she ascended the staircase with the screaming child in her arms, the heat and frustration of the past hour suddenly poured out of Amber's head. Damn that woman!—Mother. Her invasion definitely ruined the morning, and she knew exactly how to spoil an environment! How could Father have remained married to her all those years?

Amber closed the door behind her once setting Trista in her crib. The child screamed like never before. And in those moments, time froze for Amber as a surge of rage like never before felt as though it cracked the very world around her.

Such cold, foggy, windy roads; bridges that freeze and create unexpected black ice: Amber was in this landscape for a brief moment, feeling the deathly winter that howled it's fury from every direction. One could freeze to death if left injured, immobilized and isolated for many hours. Amber's rage in that moment fueled her ability to dream and fantasize the most horrible wish against Mother.

As she descended the staircase and pulled out of the daydream, Mother was alone and several miles down the rural highway. The officer had previously turned onto an intersecting road once satisfied that the woman would not return to the Dickly Castle. Mother was about to pass over a bridge with a rocky slope to a large stream below. Bridges freeze before roads. A large patch of black ice caused Mother to lose control. At 55 MPH, she slid to the right side of the highway and through a previously-damaged section of the guardrail. If there was anything fortunate that came out of this catastrophe, it was the fact that Mother didn't go over the guardrail and into water. Instead, this damaged section was at the rocky slope of the enormous ravine with the bank of the large stream below. Her car dove down the rocky slope, somersaulted a few times until the roof landed hard on the bank of the stream.

Although Mother wore her seatbelt and survived the upside-down landing, her collar bone and two arms had been badly broken. There was no way she could have pulled herself out of the driver seat and escaped through the broken, driver-side window. All she could do was lay there in excruciating pain while enduring the cold air that began to circulate in the car.

"Somebody help me! Please, somebody help me!"

In the minutes that passed, a few cars passed the area of damaged guardrail. But since the guardrail had previously been damaged, nothing appeared out of the ordinary. The overturned car, some one-hundred feet below, was unnoticeable by passing vehicles.

Back at the warm and cozy Dickly castle, Amber walked into the family room and approached Paulette. "I'm so sorry about what happened here. I'm going to let your father know about what happened once he calls. And I promise you that my mother will not be allowed in this house again; not after the trouble she caused." Amber stroked Paulette's face, "You were so brave answering that police officer's questions." She would have liked to have said, "Thank you for sticking up for me." But Paulette was only telling the truth.

"Are you okay, Honey?"

Paulette nodded her head, yes.

"Well, let's not allow my mother to ruin the plans we had for today. Trista seems to be calming down. Let me get her, and we'll put up the holiday decorations."

And so the remainder of the morning was spent as Amber wheeled out the enormous Christmas tree and placed it at the front window. By noon; mangers, Christmas angels, Santa Clause figurines, holiday candle centerpieces and even a miniature winter town that was set up under the tree all illuminated the Dickly castle and restored a sense of peace. The stereo receiver was turned to the station that played Christmas music all season long. Christmas was definitely here, and would greet Michael when he finally came home.

But several miles away, Amber's mother remained buckled in her seatbelt and upside-down in total agony from her broken bones. She shivered from the brutal cold that rushed in the broken window. And for the first time, she looked at the white-padded ceiling and noticed a pool of blood that accumulated in large drops. Somehow she had injured her head in the fall. How much blood would be lost?

"Oh my God; somebody, please help me!" Being upside-down, calling out only caused a headache.

By 1:30 in the afternoon, Amber began to think about tea for Linsey. Tea was served every day at two o'clock. Amber fit this in her mentally, auto-programmed schedule throughout week. But there was no way she would light a candle and serve tea to the statue-head; not with Michael gone! Amber wasn't particularly fond of the idol, and had no intention of adoring it when she didn't have to.

But Paulette was downstairs, and would surely take notice that the daily ritual wasn't followed. This might be communicated to Michael upon his return. It was best that Amber make afternoon tea and share some with Linsey.

By ten minutes to two o'clock, Amber lit Linsey's devotional candle. Paulette took notice of the precursor to having tea with Mother. Did Amber really have to follow this disturbing ritual? Father was gone, but Paulette would continue to endure these daily teatimes with Mother. Amber only did this to mentally torture her. This is what Paulette truly believed. Perhaps she should have told the police officer a different story that morning.

The tray with cups and teapot were brought into the living room. The first cup was poured and set beside Linsey.

Then the telephone rang.

Amber dashed over to answer it, "Hello...? Hi! You landed safely...?" Amber lifted the phone from her head and mentioned to Paulette, "Your father landed."

Then Amber carried the phone into the kitchen to continue speaking to Michael. Through the Christmas music, Paulette could pick up fragments of the phone conversation. Amber was telling Father about the morning's ordeal while apologizing.

Then several minutes later, Amber returned to the family room while continuing to talk. "Yes, I made tea. We were just going to sit down and enjoy some with Linsey."

Well that explained Amber's persistence in following the disturbing ritual

"Okay... Love you too... Call me tonight..."

After the phone call, Amber and Paulette sat in the family room while drinking tea with Linsey. Of course it was necessary for Amber to hold the cup before Paulette's lips. In these moments, she mentioned the plans for tomorrow's adventure. The family would venture to downtown Sillmac for lunch and to enjoy the Christmas lights throughout town. Sillmac lit a Christmas tree in the middle of town each year, along with a magical wonderland display of elves, Santa Clause and forest creatures. Tomorrow would be a fun outing, indeed.

But in that moment there was nothing fun at the bank of the stream, one-hundred feet below the damaged guardrail. The scene grew increasingly horrific as Amber's mother slipped in and out of consciousness. Her hands were becoming frostbitten and her body was hypothermic. The bleeding stopped from Mother's head, but this was due to a large bloodsicle that hung from her head. It managed to block the flow of blood and allow coagulation. Had it not been from the extremely freezing temperatures, Mother would have lost a great deal of blood. Darkness would fall in only a few hours. If left undiscovered overnight, surely Mother would die.

Snow in the early evening was predicted for the region of Mapleview and Sillmac. Because of this, salt trucks were dispersed along various highways and roads. And it was a driver of one of these trucks who passed along the highway near the damaged guardrail and deliberately looked over to the bank of the large stream. In milder times of the year, he often fished at that bank. But while looking over, he noticed something that certainly didn't belong there. A car was smashed up and lying overturned near the water. How long had it been there, and did someone report it? The driver of the salt truck radioed the discovery. Finally, there was some hope for Mother.

Although completely irrational, from that day forward, Mother developed an extreme fear of her daughter, Amber!

Chapter Eleven

As you know, Michael left on the 1st of December for a week's worth of business travel. But it was just one of several business trips to be had throughout December and January. And during this time, there would be some interesting activity in the Dickly castle that would remain shrouded from Michael. This interesting and shrouded activity was something that any parent should have been aware of, especially a parent of a teenage girl. Had Michael been there, he would have surely put a stop to it. But this was the first time Paulette experience a certain sense of freedom, being that she was alone with a young woman who supported her throughout the endeavor.

But for now, it was only Friday; twenty four hours after Amber's mother invaded the Dickly castle. Today was the day that Amber and her two daughters, Trista and Paulette, would spend the afternoon in downtown Sillmac.

They left the house at eleven o'clock, precisely. Paulette was bundled up warm and covered in a blanket for when she was wheeled outdoors. Little Trista wore a snowsuit, mittens and hat. She would sit on Paulette's lap, under the blanket, when going from store-to-store.

At the cafe for lunch, Amber had no problem controlling little Trista while feeding Paulette and eating her own meal. In the center of town, the three enjoyed the Christmas wonderland. Little Trista was given a chance to ride on the miniature Christmas train with all the other toddlers and small children. Of course that may have been a slight mistake. All children scream and cry when it's time to leave the ride!

That Friday afternoon was the first time Paulette had been shopping since late summer when Mother relapsed and turned deathly ill. Today, Amber stacked up a collection of the latest music CDs for Paulette, and some recent videos (DVDs didn't appear until 1995). And of course, being that Paulette was to be taken care of while Michael was gone, Amber helped her browse for some threads to add to the winter wardrobe.

The end of the outing was marked by a visit to a coffeehouse. Amber asked Paulette, "What do you usually like; mocha, cappuccino or just a plain coffee?"

Paulette shook her head, no, at each suggestion.

"Did you ever have coffee?"

Again, Paulette shook her head, no.

"Never had coffee? Oh, Honey; you need to at least try it once in your life! Let's start off with a simple cup of coffee. You don't want anything iced for today. It's too cold out."

Paulette was ordered a large mocha with plenty of sugar. "And could you put a few ice cubes in it to cool it down."

The clerk was baffled, "Ice cubes? You want ice cubes in the hot coffee?"

"Yeah, I don't want to burn her mouth and tongue!"

The clerk was still baffled as to why one would put ice cubes in coffee. It's amazing how stupid people can be at times! But he did as requested while shaking his head and mumbling all sorts of incomprehensible things that surely spoke of how weird Amber was.

When Paulette finally took her first sip, ever, of coffee; she immediately fell in love with the flavor that offered a hint of sweet chocolate. Paulette always enjoyed the smell of fresh coffee that had been brewed. She imagined it tasting absolutely wonderful. Her assumption was correct.

* * *

Coffee has a tendency to enhance our social instincts, especially for women. Back at the Dickly castle, after Friday's outing in downtown Sillmac, the sudden increase of social energy could be felt as Amber began to talk like never before. Soon she was talking about her relationship with Trista's father and how they met. "And we got along so great! He was such sweet guy, and I thought it would last forever. Well… I missed my time of the month and took a pregnancy test. The result was positive. I don't know if you know this, but you can get a false negative, but never a false positive. So I was pregnant, no doubt. I called Matt, maybe just a little nervous about how he would react. You know, even though the news might have taken him by surprise, I really think he could have been a little more supportive in that moment. He was like, 'Pregnant? Oh no? What are we going to do?' Hello? We've been going out for over a year! You love me! We talk about getting married! Maybe we do what everyone else does and have the baby and get married?"

Paulette nodded as-if in complete understanding and agreement with Amber.

Amber continued, "Well, after about a day he was more supportive and talked about getting married… maybe after the baby was born. That was fine with me; as long as he wasn't being like some of the other jerks that just leave, you know?

Well, a couple months before Trista was born, he tells me one day, 'I'm playing hockey this season.' He and his buddies usually put together a team each year and play other amateur teams throughout the area. I had a little problem with this. While he would be running around with his friends, playing hockey, our baby was going to be born. I needed him to be around, be a father, support us and stuff. Not that there's anything wrong with playing hockey, but I needed him to grow up at that moment and not play that season."

Amber sighed before continuing, "Towards the end of the pregnancy I was seeing him less and less. A couple days would go by without a phone call. I knew something was up. Sure enough, I hear that he's got some girlfriend out there. I asked him about it, but he denied it. 'Where have you been these past couple days?' 'Oh, I've just been busy with work and playing hockey and stuff.' Yeah, right; don't give me your crap!

He never actually broke up with me. He came to the hospital after I delivered, congratulated me and said he had to get to work and would visit later. But I never saw him after that."

Couldn't Mother and Father have encouraged Amber to pursue child support from her boyfriend?

Suddenly, Amber realized that Paulette could have never had a boyfriend. Outside of immediate family and friends, the poor girl never experienced love or the ups and downs of dating. "Listen to me, complaining about my past love life! You probably never had the chance to go out on a date. Have you ever had a boyfriend?"

Paulette shook her head, no, with a disappointed look.

"Awe, I'm sorry, Honey! I wonder if there's a way to get you hooked up with someone."

In the present day, television commercials boast highly successful websites that bring lovers together. In fact, statistics demonstrate that the percentage of marriages brought about by online dating is steadily increasing. Throughout the 90s, however, finding a lover on the computer was an activity not to be proud of. It was similar to browsing personal ads, except worse! People looking for a relationship online were believed to be losers, nerds, ugly people, handicapped; or people who were alone for good reason and hid behind the computer screen. This wasn't entirely true, of course! But it was the common belief in the early 90s.

Amber was an intelligent, young woman. She felt that although no "decent catch" could be found online, she believed that such interaction for Paulette would fuel and spark the necessary fantasies for her to have some experience with romance. What harm could it have done to give a sixteen-year-old, paralyzed girl a long-distance boyfriend? If all went well, she could read love letters from her long distance romance on the computer screen, and peck out her replies with pencil in mouth. It was harmless from what Amber believed.

"Paulette, I've heard about people who find a relationship online; with the computer, you know?"

Paulette maintained her usual, blank stare; but with a hint of confusion. What on Earth could Amber have been suggesting?

"I've never been online, myself; but I hear that people can hook up for love and dating. It's usually long distance, and the communication is done over email. What if we found you a nice boyfriend?"

Paulette smiled and began to giggle. Just as with crying, vocal words are not necessary for laughter as the reaction is instinctive.

This surprised Amber, "You're laughing! You can laugh?"

Paulette nodded while her giggle toned down to a wide smile.

Amber continued with her suggestion, "Seriously, we can get a nice picture of you sitting on the couch. You're very pretty, just like your mother. We can write up a nice ad for you, saying that you're a lonely girl looking for friendship and someone to talk to. But we better say that you're eighteen. There might be some legal issues if you are a minor. What do you say?"

Paulette beamed from ear-to-ear while nodding, yes.

And so on that afternoon, Paulette was dolled up extra pretty with makeup to accentuate her already beautiful features that resembled her mother's. Her hair was styled with a slight curl.

She sat propped up on the sofa while Amber took a photo with Michael's expensive, digital camera that provided a means to upload photos onto the computer. This was cutting edge in 1994, and *very* expensive!

In the distance on one of the side tables, Linsey observed a situation that could easily harm Paulette. What was Amber doing?

The two young women returned to Paulette's bedroom and dialed up online. Remember the tones and the annoying squeals as a computer would connect to the Internet? Limited to a collection of icons such as news, shopping, business and entertainment; Amber searched until finding a section called Personals/Dating.

"Lonely, small town girl in search of a nice guy for conversation, friendship and possibly more." Amber hit the backspace button to erase "and possibly more", as this might have suggested the wrong thing to whoever was out there. She looked at Paulette, "We don't want you to seem desperate."

Paulette's photo was finally uploaded, and the entire ad submitted so that it could be browsed by whoever was out there.

* * *

Michael called that evening, as he would do throughout the entire week of his absence. With Trista and Paulette sleeping upstairs, Amber sat in the family room on the cozy sofa where she and Michael made out on Thanksgiving night. At least his voice was with her, enough to allow further acquainting of the man she loved. But after an hour it was necessary for Michael to retire for the evening. When he traveled on business, it was necessary to rest up for the following day. But he reminded Amber the days remaining before he returned. He would do this every night as the days remaining reduced in number.

Now alone, Amber turned on the large-screen TV and flipped through the channels. But she couldn't help but notice that blasted statue-head of Linsey. Amber thought to herself, "Would you like to retire and go to bed for the night, Linsey?" Poor Linsey certainly looked tired, appearing to have wished for nothing more than to rest her weary head on the pillows. But Amber wouldn't dare touch the statue-head, or carry it upstairs. What if she dropped it and broke it? Michael could never forgive her!

Trying to focus on the TV screen, Amber couldn't help but notice that Linsey continued to glare at her. At some point, Amber could actually feel it, as-if a real person was in that room and maintaining an intent gaze. Linsey wasn't tired or wishing to go to bed. Linsey had a serious bone of contention with Amber!

This was Amber's family room, now! It was *her* house and *her* man. Although Amber would never claim Paulette to be exclusively hers and no longer Linsey's, she had it in her heart to be the motherly figure, maybe even earn the name of Mom. Linsey had no right to dictate to Amber of what was right or what shouldn't be done. And Amber had quite enough of Linsey's presence. She stood up, walked to the kitchen and pulled a clean dishtowel from one of the drawers. The dishtowel wasn't large enough to cover Linsey's entire head. Instead, Amber draped it over the statue's forehead so that Linsey's face would be covered.

Finally, Amber was the woman in the home. Of course the dishtowel would be removed in the morning before Paulette came downstairs.

Chapter Twelve

It wasn't such an inconvenience for Amber to quickly run downstairs in the morning and remove Linsey's veil from her face. "Good morning, Linsey. It's nice to have you with us today." Already Amber was establishing that the house and family belonged to her. Linsey was merely a guest, but certainly welcome.

The usual routines were followed for the morning; changing Trista's diaper, giving her a bottle, washing Paulette and dressing her. And breakfast was made for Amber's girls; French toast with bacon along with freshly squeezed orange juice. Yes, Amber was a fine mother and housewife who could care for the home and children so very well.

One could easily see that Paulette had something on her mind. It was almost as-if she anticipated in uncontrollable excitement.

Amber smiled, "Just look at you! You want to go upstairs and see if you have any messages from the online dating.—don't you?"

Paulette smiled and nodded in return.

"Alright, let me clean up after breakfast and we'll go back up to the computer."

Fifteen minutes later, the wheelchair was loaded on the lift so that Paulette could return to her bedroom. Once upstairs, Amber dialed online and opened Paulette's mailbox.

"Ha! You've got a message!"

Excitement glistened in Paulette's eyes.

The header of the email, delivered from the online dating site, provided a summary of the interested person. Amber read the key items. "Let's see… twenty-nine years old… occupation, electrical engineer… interested in women, friendship and dating. He's not bad looking, either!" Amber turned the monitor towards Paulette so that she could view the profile picture. He was a good-looking guy; no one that Amber would have been interested in. But for Paulette, it was a guy who had interest in her advertisement and probably her profile image. The morning definitely had some excitement for Paulette.

"Do you want to go ahead and read his message?" Amber scrolled down to the opening paragraph of the email.

Paulette nodded, yes.

Both women read the message on the screen that served as a brief introduction and an invitation to continue correspondence. "Hi, my name is Todd. I'm 29 years old and I work as an electrical engineer at a robotics development company. But don't let my career fool you into thinking that I'm some kind of nerd. I'm into bodybuilding, martial arts, and spend my weekends cruising the highways in my ninja crotch-rocket. I'm looking for someone to sit behind me and enjoy the roads and scenery.

I saw your picture and your ad. You definitely seem like someone I would like to get to know, hopefully be your friend—maybe more. I'm looking forward to hearing from you.

Todd"

Paulette provided a look that suggested being unsure of what to do next.

"Well, do you like the guy? Would you want to make him your pen pal?"

Paulette nodded her head, yes; but still maintained a look for guidance.

As for Amber, she pieced together her initial impressions of Todd. Throughout his introductory email, Amber thought to herself that although not a bad-looking guy who looked slightly toned from exercise and cruised around on his motorcycle, he apparently had problems maintaining—possibly starting—relationships with the opposite sex. Why else would he have been seeking romance online? There should have been plenty of women to choose from where he lived. The fact that Todd was an electrical engineer, and the fact that he insisted, "Don't let my career fool you into thinking that I'm some kind of nerd." suggested to Amber that perhaps Todd was a once-nerd who had gone badass—more like gone attempted badass as she could sense an exaggerated, self-perception from his email. It's such a shame that we draw conclusions and judge a book on its cover based on prejudices. And it's such a disappointment to know that someone like Amber would have labeled a guy like Todd in a harsh, cynical way. But her impressions weren't entirely cruel. She also assumed him to be a good-natured person, simply hid behind his struggle to maintain an image of something that he was not. Amber further concluded that both Todd and Paulette had some obstacles in life that prevented them from enjoying a relationship with the opposite sex. The two were good for one another, at least in the provided limited medium. Aside from that, Amber believed that Todd couldn't hurt Paulette. He lived hundreds of miles away. How could he possibly hurt a teenage girl through nothing more than words?

"Well, whatever you do, never give him your address or telephone number; okay?"

Paulette nodded.

"And you don't want to seem desperate or too eager to strike up a friendship with him. Let the guy work a little for you. Why don't we just tell him something like, 'Thanks for responding to my ad… You seem like a really, nice guy… I'd be interested in hearing more about you…' Stuff like that. You know what I mean?"

Paulette nodded.

"Do you want to write it out yourself?" This meant that Paulette would peck the reply on the keyboard with pencil in mouth, and then hit the send button.

Again, Paulette nodded.

"Ok, but don't say anything about your physical condition just yet. You don't want to give too many details." Amber paused for a moment before continuing, "Do you think we should keep this a secret from your dad?"

Paulette provided a blank expression that gradually turned into, "I never thought of that." Then she slowly nodded her head, yes. Surely, Father wouldn't have allowed such a correspondence.

And so Paulette pecked out her initial reply to Todd, being careful not to seem too eager as Amber suggested, but leaving the door open for further correspondence. She was still unsure and unfamiliar with the situation, and did exactly as Amber suggested. But surely it would only be a matter of time before Paulette's emotions made her very familiar with the situation and desiring so much more. Amber had no idea how things were about to spiral out of control.

* * *

The following morning, after breakfast, Paulette's wheelchair was loaded on the lift so she could return to her bedroom and check for an email from Todd. Amber dialed online which was followed by the annoying scream and pulses of the modem.

"Ha! You've got an email!" Amber took the liberty to open the message from Todd and read the few paragraphs in silence, just to see what sort of communication he intended with Paulette. It was merely some more details of his background; education, where he attended college, where he was working. And then he went on to explain the much heartache and disappointment that was experienced through dating. According to him, it appeared that women were unable to appreciate a guy with a "heart of gold". Todd was hoping that becoming acquainted with a nice girl across the miles and online would prove successful.

Todd didn't seem like such a bad guy to Amber. "Well, he's nice. He has my approval. Tell you what; from now on, I'm going to let you have your privacy. Those emails are addressed to you and I won't bother reading them. But if you need help with anything, just let me know."

Chapter Thirteen

Exactly one week from the day that Michael left, he returned to the Dickly castle. It was Thursday afternoon at a half-past one o'clock. The small family sat in the family room, waiting for the appearance of a limousine or the possible sound of a toot from a musical horn that would announce Michael's arrival. Although Paulette was eager to see her father after his weeklong absence, she had other things on her mind; in particular, her boyfriend who had written her every day from hundreds of miles away. Paulette would have never imagined that her soul mate was truly out there and destined to meet her through (what was considered at the time) the unusual medium of the Internet. And although she maintained her physical condition a secret from Todd, hope continued to live in her heart that her soul mate would accept the obstacle in their love.

While waiting for her future husband to return, Amber glanced over to Linsey to ensure that the dishtowel used to cover her face each night was not nearby. Tea with Linsey was followed every afternoon, so the book of matches and candle were in their rightful places. But Amber couldn't help but look upon Linsey with jealousy. Although Amber and Michael would surely do some much needed cuddling and romance that night, Michael would most-likely sleep with Linsey afterwards. How much longer would Amber have to endure the competition?

Amber suddenly announced to Paulette, "I suppose your father will want to have tea promptly at two o'clock. I'll make some."

While Amber left the family room for the kitchen, Little Trista remained near the monstrous Christmas tree, playing with the ornaments that dangled from the bottom. In recent days, it was necessary to rearrange the ornaments at the bottom of the tree so that no breakables would suffer at the hands of the little one. The entire house was decorated for Christmas; lit and waiting to greet Michael with holiday cheer.

As the burner was ignited underneath the teapot, the musical toot of the limousine horn could be heard. Michael was home! Amber ran into the grand foyer and was seconds from opening the entry door. But she turned towards the family room and whispered out to Paulette, "Remember, don't say anything to your father about your boyfriend!"

Paulette nodded from across the room. Amber was more than a mother; she was a friend who could keep a secret.

The door was opened as Michael approached from the horseshoe driveway, so handsome in his business suit with trench coat draped across his arm. Behind him the limousine driver unloaded the luggage.

When lovers lock eyes their pupils dilate, and the whites nearly radiate a soft pink with an unmistakable glisten. A week apart was such a long time. Michael and Amber embraced so that their beating hearts would finally touch. And how good it felt to be in Michael's warm, loving arms and to receive his kiss.

"You decorated the house."

"Uh-huh; do you like it?"

"It's beautiful; you did a great job."

Then Michael announced, "Where's that daughter of mine?" Surely she was in the family room, waiting for Father's return. He entered while taking sight of his teary-eyed girl. Paulette was happy for his return. It had been his first trip away since Mother died.

"So I trust everything went well while I was gone?"

Amber reassured Michael that everything was fine, but he kept his eyes on Paulette as she nodded in agreement with Amber.

Amber continued, "We went out last Friday for lunch in Sillmac... visited the winter wonderland in town... shopped for some winter clothes for Paulette, CDs and some movies..."

"Good!" Michael turned his attention back to Amber. "It sounds like you ladies got along really well." Then he glanced over towards little Trista who stood near the Christmas tree. "And how's the little one been?"

"Oh, we had to rearrange the Christmas tree. She loves playing with the ornaments."

Just then, the teapot whistled on the stove.

Amber exclaimed, "Oh, the water is ready. I was just making afternoon tea." She walked back into the kitchen and prepared the tray with teacups as she did every afternoon. While doing this, Amber had to wonder if Michael and Paulette exchanged secret conversation of whispers along with nods of Paulette's head and blinks of her eyes. What would Paulette mention of the week alone with Amber? Outside of Paulette's secret boyfriend, Amber believed she had nothing to fear.

Several minutes later, the family sat in the family room while tea bags steeped in cups of hot water. A candle was lit near Linsey as usual with the first cup offered to her.

Michael brought in his briefcase and mentioned gifts for everyone. "Now ladies; it isn't Christmas, yet. This is just a little something to let you know I had been thinking of you."

A small box was brought over to Paulette and opened. She smiled and looked up to her father as if to say, "Thank you". It was a small Christmas tree pendant, slightly decorated with jewels as the ornaments and lights. Secured to a thin, gold chain;

Michael placed the holiday jewelry around his daughter's neck. "There, now you look like you're in the Christmas spirit!"

Michael returned to the briefcase and reached in a plastic bag for a stuffed animal kitty. "Trista?"

She knew there was some surprise at the mention of her name.

"Look what I got for you!" He extended the adorable stuffed animal towards the child while bringing it to life by slightly tilting the kitty's head.

Trista was delighted as she smiled and quickly toddled towards Michael. Finally hugging the soft, furry toy was the only way she understood of how to take it.

Finally, a small box was presented to Amber. She opened it to reveal a set of earrings that may have been similar to Paulette's pendant. They were two, small Christmas trees, decorated with tiny jewels. The earrings were small enough to be modestly displayed on the lobes.

"You have your ears pierced, right? At least I think I noticed them being pierced?"

"Yes and thank you! They're beautiful." Amber stood up and kissed Michael, followed by a hug.

* * *

Late in the evening, after Trista and Paulette had gone to bed, Michael and Amber sat in their usual places on the sofa, cuddling to the sounds of the evening news that softly murmured in the distance. Amber's new earrings were in. She was sure to proudly display them before dinner.

"I sat here every night while talking to you on the phone. Tonight, you are finally back."

Michael gave his young and beautiful Amber a kiss. He missed her equally the same while he was gone. But there was some sad news that would break the warm and fuzzy mood of lovers reuniting. Michael sighed, "I'm going to have to go out of town again in a couple of weeks. I'll be leaving on the 19th, but will be sure to return by the 23rd. That'll be the Friday before Christmas Eve. After that, there won't be any travel until after the first of the year."

Amber was disappointed, "Again...?" But she understood that Michael had a business to run.

"Yes, again; I'm sorry. It's just the nature of my job. It requires meeting people and travel. A lot of people seem to think that a job like this is bad for a marriage. Linsey and I stayed close all those years. It just takes commitment and patience along with making every moment together quality time."

Amber smiled and probably flushed near the cheeks. Michael's mention of marriage was probably unintentional. He was only citing an example of a romantic relationship that survived through his years of running the company, and hoped it would apply to the current romance. But what if? What if he was implying something more? Amber wasn't about to raise her hopes beyond their current elevation. She only reassured her future husband, "I'll be sure to make every moment with you quality. And I know your job requires travel."

Michael would certainly need her services as housekeeper and mother to Paulette. But just to verify, Amber briefly asked, "Same deal as before? You want me to stay here with Paulette?"

"Of course! And I want you to keep the house nice and warm for me when I return."

For the young woman of only twenty-two, it was the greatest moment of love, ever. But it was harshly interrupted after Michael's sudden reminder, "Linsey will continue to watch over things while I'm gone. Which reminds me..." Michael pulled from his warm cuddle with Amber and stood up from the sofa. "I got something for Linsey, too." There were some remaining bags at the grand foyer which hadn't been removed since Michael returned home that afternoon. In one of the bags were two bottle of Pinot Noir, Linsey's favorite. Wasn't that nice of Michael to remember a gift for his deceased wife?

And of course a bottle was opened with the first glass poured for Linsey. As usual, Michael and Amber would enjoy a glass-and-a half of Pinot Noir; and whatever Linsey wouldn't finish, it would be dumped down the drain. It is, after all, unbecoming to drink another's unfinished glass of wine.

Amber wasn't there to get drunk, anyway. The wine merely an added dimension to soft light, warm cuddling and loving conversation. She usually ignored the presence of the statue-head and ignored Michael's private fantasies of continuing to share his life with a deceased person. The only thing that mattered in that moment was the warm bond between her and Michael that grew stronger every day.

Michael had been gone for over a week. He and Amber had much catching up to do in the department of late night romance. Soon they lay beside one another; kissing, touching, fondling and loving. He was so lucky to have her, a near replica of the Linsey of years ago. It was almost as-if Michael transported himself back in time to relive those days when he and Linsey were young. Of course Michael was much, more refined now than in his younger years; able to offer things such as gifts and money that he couldn't when Linsey was young. Unbeknown to the young Linsey who lay beside Michael, she had a teenage daughter who slept upstairs. And she lay on the sofa of her own home, a castle that sat on a small mountain in Sillmac. It's amazing what the mind can do if allowed. Exactly what is reality?

But she wasn't Linsey, Michael knew that. A fleeting fantasy or two never hurt anyone. Soon he returned to reality where a beautiful, young woman lay with him and very, much in love with him. And of course Michael loved his Amber more and more each day. She was the best thing that could have happened since Linsey died. But he wasn't quite ready to let go of his deceased wife.

"Well, I suppose we should call it a night. Let's go out for breakfast in the morning."

Amber lay there with her face near his, eyes deeply fixed into Michael's and a soft smile with a glow. She wouldn't dare ask or appear to desire. But how she wished to have gone up to his room for the night, shared the bed and felt the warmth of his body.

Instead, that blasted statue-head of Linsey was carefully picked up and given a kiss to its cheek. "Well Linsey, it's been over a week since you've been to bed."

There would be no further good night kisses for Amber and Michael as they went their separate ways for the night—not with Linsey in Michael's hands!

He was improving; this is how Amber felt at the moment. In a more extreme case, Michael would have pulled out the bottles of Pinot Noir that afternoon and showed them to Linsey—maybe even talked to her, "See what I got you, Linsey?" Instead, Michael kept the bottles in the grand foyer and brought them out at a more appropriate moment. Aside from that, it had only been a little over two months since Michael lost his wife. Amber was in an extremely rare situation. How lucky she was to not only be involved in a romantic relationship with Michael, but to live in his house and care for matters while he went away on business. Amber would gladly sleep in the guest room until the time was right.

* * *

Despite the romance and soft mood of the previous evening, along with mentions of maintaining commitment and patience—not to mention a slip of possible marriage from Michael—the following morning was a bit on the cold and unfriendly side. In fact, the following morning was as-if the previous evening never occurred.

This was a morning when the family was to go out for breakfast. Michael made mention of it the previous evening. Awakening at her usual time, Amber noticed that Trista remained sleeping which could have provided Amber a jump start on caring for Paulette. She quietly stepped out of the guest bedroom and immediately noticed the aroma of coffee hanging in the air. Michael was certainly downstairs, and there wasn't anyone Amber would have like to see more than the man she was so in love with. She lightly walked down the stairs and turned at the main level towards the kitchen. There Michael stood with a cup of coffee, looking out the kitchen window at the cold, early morning.

"Hi! Good morning!" Amber greeted softly, nearly whispering.

"Hey…" is all that Michael said.

It was still early. Maybe he needed his coffee. Amber approached and lightly rubbed her palm on his muscular back that was covered by a t-shirt. But he wasn't so receptive to her touch. What could have been wrong? Amber pulled her hand away and back to her own side.

Finally, Michael spoke. "I'm going to ask you something."

"Sure…"

"Is Paulette okay?"

"Sure, Paulette's been fine. We got along great while you were gone. Why do you ask?"

"I don't know; something tells me that Paulette is having some trouble. I really need to get to the bottom of it, and I thought I would ask you. So is everything okay with her?"

Amber was speechless. Did Michael find out about Paulette's boyfriend? Did he talk to her earlier? Maybe she made something up to her father? It suddenly felt as though answering questions was dangerous. Maybe it was best to remain vague. "She seemed healthy and her usual self while you were gone. I stuck to the daily routine, and she hung out with me throughout the day. Michael, what's wrong? What makes you think Paulette is in trouble?"

The look on Michael's face was that of not trusting Amber and of not believing her. "I just want to make sure that if anything was wrong with Paulette, you would tell me."

"Michael, of course! You have to believe me! She seemed fine the whole week!"

Michael remained silent; topped off his cup of coffee; walked past Amber, up the stairs and into his office where the door was shut.

It was a moment of extreme crisis for Amber. She failed and disappointed the man she loved. It was difficult not to panic while speculating the many possibilities. The only explanation for the moment was Paulette. Somehow Paulette must have communicated a wrongdoing of Amber's or something that she felt was mistreatment. The only natural course of action would have been to carefully approach Paulette on the matter. The seconds ticked away, and perhaps Amber's time was running out in the Dickly castle. It was best to do this now.

But Trista was calling out from her crib. There was now the responsibility of changing her night time diaper and fixing a bottle. And even while Trista finally lay by herself on Paulette's bed, drinking her morning bottle, it was necessary to wait for Paulette to finish her morning business. Everyone needs to relieve themselves after a night of sleep, and should do so unbothered.

After Paulette completed her morning business and was lowered into the tub, Amber sat down at the side and quietly spoke. "Paulette, I want to ask you something, and I really need an honest answer."

Paulette's eyes spoke with truth in that moment as she nodded her head, yes. Whatever Amber needed, she would surely tell her. The two had gotten very close in recent weeks.

"Paulette, did you tell your father about your boyfriend?"

Paulette's eyes opened wide as she nodded her head, no.

"No? Did he talk to you about me, maybe ask how I am doing?"

Again, Paulette shook her head, no.

This was very strange for Amber. She was an intelligent, young woman with a strong sense of intuition. As far as Amber could see, the girl was telling the truth. So what might have alarmed Michael of Paulette's well being? Then again, maybe Paulette was a good actor.

The girl sensed Amber's sudden doubt and mistrust. She would have to wait until fully dressed and waiting to have her hair blow-dried so that she could turn to the computer and monitor, indicating a need to say something.

When that time came, Amber rolled the cart over and stuck a pencil in Paulette's mouth. Was she going to confess? Was she going to give a warning?

"Why would I tell my father? He would never let me have Todd! Why don't you believe me?"

The girl was right. This boyfriend of hers meant too much, and she certainly wouldn't jeopardize the relationship by telling Father. "I'm sorry, Paulette. I believe you now. I'm just really scared. Your father was asking me some serious questions, like I had done something wrong to you. He never came up to you in private and asked about me?"

"No. Nothing."

"What about being able to see your emails? Can he log in? Does he have your password?"

"No, he doesn't go online. He has no reason to. He probably wouldn't know how." This was true for the early 90s. Believe it or not, a business could be run without email and the Internet. Of course a few years later, these things would be a necessity.

Although frightened and in a panic, Amber had a way to see things so very clearly in that moment. Michael had seen nothing on his computer. Paulette had spoken not one word about her boyfriend, or mentioned any false wrongdoings of Amber. In fact nothing alive or physically noticeable had caused Michael to be suspicious of Amber. It was the blasted statue-head of Linsey! Somehow the relic had the power to bring clairvoyance to Michael. Linsey warned her Earthly husband overnight of a possible danger, and it involved Amber.

Chapter Fourteen

After a day-or-so, Michael returned to his usual self. One might have assumed his sudden mistrust of Amber to be only misdirected guilt. He was so much in love with Amber, and it had only been a little over two months since Linsey's death. How else should a grieving husband react in such a difficult time?

But Amber knew better! Perhaps Michael did believe he had a spell of misguided guilt and made a conscious effort to correct this. And it was good for Amber that Michael made this erroneous conclusion. She knew very well that Linsey warned her Earthly husband of his new lover. And perhaps Linsey was right in doing so. Maybe Amber wasn't acting responsibly during Michael's absence. Perhaps allowing Paulette to have an online romance wasn't in the teenage girl's best interest. Amber considered these things, and decided that going forward, she would "filter" the emails to Paulette; briefly skim through the long-distance love letters for anything that would be considered objectionable.

As was the usual daily ritual, Paulette would return to her bedroom after breakfast and allow Amber to dial up online. But one December morning, while Michael was still home and a couple weeks from leaving for his next trip, Amber sat down with Paulette for a brief talk before checking email.

"I'm not trying to get into your business, but I'm going to start skimming your emails from Todd, just to make sure he isn't trying to hurt you or anything."

Paulette maintained a blank stare in return.

"It'll just help keep my conscience clear. I'm supposed to be taking care of you while your father is gone. Well, instead I'm letting you talk to a stranger online. Again, I'm going to stay out of your business as best as I can, but I want to briefly screen your emails, that's all. Please try to understand."

Paulette really had no choice in the matter. She was paralyzed and dependent on Amber for many things. All she could do was go along with the new rule.

As expected, an email from Todd was in Paulette's mailbox. Amber opened it to quickly skim through before turning the computer cart towards Paulette. There wasn't anything out of the ordinary with the email. In fact, it was quite boring. Most of the email was Todd's self-praising of himself for another great workout completed at the gym and how he pumped his biceps. The workout was followed by a lengthy cruise in his ninja-style crotch rocket, and then wrapped up with a couple beers at home. Then he mentioned some friction between himself and a coworker, revealing a secret need to lash out all those things learned at the dojo (martial arts school) on his coworker. Todd had a black belt in some kind of martial arts and felt it was his duty to "teach people lessons" who didn't know how to respect others. From what Amber could make of it, Todd was being a bit unfair and immature with the office conflict. It was only a silly misunderstanding between him and a coworker. No wonder Todd was single!

The email concluded with a final, two-sentence paragraph, mentioning how great it was that Paulette's father had given her a nice pendant. It was the only interaction in the email between Todd and Paulette. Paulette was nothing more than a diary for Todd that might have occasionally responded to his daily stories and self-praise. How boring! Maybe Paulette would grow tired of the one-sided relationship.

"Okay, it seems like a safe email to me. I don't know what I'm worried about." Paulette was left alone to read.

Of course Amber would continue to skim the boring emails that were written by a pathetically, self-absorbed nerd-gone-macho. It was all done for Linsey in hopes that Michael would receive no further warnings.

And then came the morning of December 19th, the day when Michael was scheduled to leave for another business trip, to be home by the 23rd. More money was given to Amber (as-if she didn't have enough already!) followed by hugs and kisses to Amber and Paulette before leaving in the limousine.

Being that the family stayed downstairs with Michael after breakfast, it was necessary for poor Paulette to wait until after eleven o'clock in the morning to finally read her anticipated, daily email from Todd. Amber loaded her onto the wheelchair lift and brought the girl upstairs. Then Amber dialed up online like every morning and opened the mailbox to read another boring email from Todd.

But today's email was not boring! After the first paragraph, Amber's jaw dropped as she turned to Paulette and asked, "Has he ever sent you something like this before?"

Paulette had yet to read the daily email from Todd and didn't have a clue as to what Amber referred to.

"No… No, no, no; I'm not going to let you see this!"

The look provided by Paulette questioned Amber, "What right do you have to withhold an email from my boyfriend?"

This took Amber off guard. How was she going to handle a situation like this? It was Amber's duty to filter the emails and ensure that nothing harmful would reach Paulette. But on the other hand, she could see the demand in Paulette's eyes to read the email. "Okay; look, I can't keep you from seeing this. All I'm going to say is that you might not want to read an email like this. Have you ever heard of Pandora's Box?"

Agitated, Paulette nodded her head, yes.

"Honey, that's what this is! If you read this, there'll be no turning back. I actually think it might be cruel if I showed this to you."

Paulette insisted with an intense, demanding look. And despite how against Amber was with email, she turned the computer cart towards Paulette. Surely, Linsey rolled over in her grave at that moment!

Before describing the email of that morning, it's best for the reader to understand the sort of individuals who existed on the Internet back in the early 1990s. Today, in modern times, if you happen to enter the wrong sort of social area on the Internet—such as a filthy, lowlife chat room—you will encounter nothing more than tasteless messages that reveal immature perceptions of sex.

I suppose if you are one of those women who have an uncontrollable, instinctive desire to suddenly add thug to your family gene pool, then you might respond to such a message; to which you would soon receive demands for nude photos of yourself, maybe a video or web cam of you performing shameful acts on yourself. If you are lucky, the interested person might actually want to meet you in real life. And I suppose if you wish for STDs or perhaps an abnormal spawn of such a thug, then you might take him up on the offer.

But in the early 1990s, computers weren't exactly a common household appliance like they are today. It was most often educated people and those who could afford such a luxury that owned a computer and went online. But don't fool yourself! Sex happens in every time and in every place. Sex certainly did happen online in the early 1990s, and it was done in the form of emails with descriptive paragraphs that were crafted to titillate the other party. And there were even individuals such as Todd, who could have easily qualified as trashy romance novelists.

Todd's introductory email of erotica was a suggestion to take the online correspondence to the next level. It was his attempt to reach across the hundreds of miles and create a nearly-tangible reality where he and Paulette could exist in.

Paulette's face blushed throughout several parts of the email, reading of how her boyfriend would kiss her passionately, touch and explore various parts of her body, and just about everything else that a paralyzed girl shouldn't have read or imagined.

What had Amber done? This was so cruel! Surely Paulette was incapable of extinguishing any desire after reading such an erotic email. And to make matters worse, she would surely respond to Todd with a little story of her own. But did Paulette have any idea of the consequences? It would be pure torture for the girl. Amber was going to have to act quickly!

Mother and Father would have never assisted Paulette in that capacity. And in no way was Amber going to help, either! Aside from that, no one probably mentioned the act to Paulette. Who would teach her?

Well that was a silly question! No one is ever taught how to do it! Simply out of basic need, all creatures figure out their own technique. But while considering these things, Amber asked herself, "If I was paralyzed from the neck, down, how could I do it? Even more, can a paralyzed person feel it?"

Later that evening, while tucking Paulette in bed, Amber presented a most-strange item that one wouldn't immediately associate with bedtime. But as Amber described, this item could be useful late at night. It was one of those backscratchers that Father purchased at a souvenir shop while on vacation. Amber altered the souvenir so that a doll rod extension had been secured to the handle with electrical tape.

"You know Paulette, the other night I was laying in bed and thought of you. I had gotten a bad itch on my leg and immediately scratched it. Then I realized that you wouldn't be able to do this, not with your condition. So I found this for you and added the extension so it can be held in your mouth and used to scratch whatever you want. I'm going to tuck it under the covers with you and lay it on your pillow. That way, if you ever have a terrible itch, say maybe near your thigh or someplace, you can put the handle in your mouth and scratch where it is needed."

Paulette returned the queerest look! What in the world was Amber talking about?

"Use it for when you have an itch under the blanket. Don't you sometimes get an itch under the blanket?"

Paulette maintained her queer look.

"I'll leave it for you under the covers. You'll never know when you might need it most." Amber turned out the light and left Paulette alone for the evening.

Did Amber really believe she solved everything? While Amber sat alone in the family room, waiting for Michael to call, Linsey glared from a distance in bitter disbelief. How dare Amber allow Paulette to read a dirty email addressed to her? How dare she even allow the girl to continue communication with the creep? And how dare Amber suggest to Paulette that she begin masturbating in the late night hours?

Amber had quite enough of Linsey's criticism. Had it not been for Amber, Paulette would have never experienced what it felt like to be in love. And why shouldn't Paulette be allowed to feel pleasure? Being that the poor girl was paralyzed, masturbation might have been the only thing that could accelerate her heart and improve circulation.

Where was that dishtowel? Oh, that's right; Amber put Linsey's cover away while Michael was home. It was time to remind the deceased woman of who ran the house and family. Amber went into the kitchen for a new dishtowel, and returned to the family room where it was draped over Linsey's face. Peace and quiet was restored to the family room.

Before starting the morning, before even going into Paulette's room to ready the paralyzed girl for the day, Amber was always sure to remove the dishtowel from Linsey's face. The last thing Amber would have wanted was for Paulette to mention any disrespect for the relic. Little did Amber know that Paulette would have been happy for the thing to be out of view. But as was the custom of every morning in Michael's absence, Amber softly descended the stairs to the main level where she turned to the family room and over to Linsey.

This morning was different! While halfway down the stairway, Amber heard the most frightening sound that resembled that of vicious growling. But it was the sort of crackled growling that one might hear in a zombie movie when a corpse has come back to life after some years. Vocal chords would have been void of any moisture or lubrication in all those years. Any vicious growling would have sounded like eerie, dry whispers.

The sounds were definitely downstairs on the main level. And as Amber drew close to the family room; the cracked, dry-whispered growling became all the louder. Finally at the entry of the family room, Amber began to suspect that the noises were coming from Linsey!

Amber wished she could have laughed at her ridiculous conclusion. In no way would a statue come to life and begin growling behind a cover. Amber's approach grew all the slower until she stood before the covered statue-head and carefully extended her arm towards it. Did she really want to expose the face? What was behind the cover?

Amber did the unthinkable! Despite her moment of terror and full knowledge of the noises' origination, she pulled the dishtowel off Linsey. Linsey's face was contorted with rage. Her eyes were open and nearly burning with fury. Teeth were exposed like some vicious animal as Linsey snarled at the woman she hated most.

Amber's scream awoke her from the terrifying nightmare. Thank goodness it was only a bad dream! She turned to the nightstand and could see that it was only 2:11 in the morning. Little Trista remained sleeping, undisturbed from Mommy's scream in the night.

Where-as most people in this situation would lay paralyzed with fear and consider that perhaps matters were in much need of correction; Amber only lay in the dark with increased resentment towards Linsey. She knew that Linsey was communicating through the relic and did not approve of Amber's approach as woman of the household.

But as far as Amber was concerned, all fornications should have been extended to Linsey. She was thoroughly fed up with the woman's meddling and how she stirred mistrust in Michael. And now she had problems with Paulette's freedom to enjoy a boyfriend? The girl couldn't be sheltered forever!

The following morning, Amber went downstairs—fully awake this time. The dishtowel was removed from Linsey's face and it remained nothing more than a stationary replica of a woman who once was. But how much longer would Amber have to do battle with thing?

Chapter Fifteen

Poor Linsey: her days were numbered at the Dickly castle, and her final hour had neared. True, the young Amber lived in fear and resentment of Linsey's presence and wondered how much longer she would be confronted with something that would not die. But it's a good thing Amber maintained her poise during those moments. As she would soon find out, the relic would no longer torment her.

It all began Friday afternoon, December 23rd when Michael returned from his business trip to be home for the Christmas holiday. The holiday would extend through New Years, of course, to be followed by additional business some time after the first of the year. But for now, Michael was home for the holidays with full intent to enjoy the happiest time of the year with his family.

He came home just in time for afternoon tea with Linsey. During those moments, Michael discussed with Amber and Paulette of the best time to go to church for Christmas.

When Linsey was alive, church was every Sunday along with Easter, Christmas, Ash Wednesday and Good Friday. Although not following other days of holy obligation such as All Saints Day, Linsey saw to it that her family was a God-loving, Christian family with a strong sense of morality. Church was an important event each week, whether Michael was home or on business.

But what of Amber? As the new woman of the house, did she encourage this? Considering that Michael, Paulette and Amber hadn't been to church since the funeral, anyone's guess would be, no. As for Amber's personal devotion before the funeral, she hadn't been to church since little Trista's baptism. And before that, God only knows.

Such a heathen; Amber now excitedly spoke of attending church on Christmas Eve with Linsey's husband and daughter. "Do they have a mass in the late afternoon?"

Michael replied, "They do; usually around four o'clock. Maybe we'll go to that one and then come back home to begin our Christmas celebration." Michael looked over to his daughter, "Oh, Amber doesn't know about our yearly tradition!" Then he turned his attention back to Amber. "On Christmas Eve we have cold, smoked salmon from Saulmon's along with shrimp cocktail, cheese and other things. It's Paulette's favorite meal of the year. She loves shrimp cocktail. Saulmon's should be open in the morning. I'll be sure to pick up the salmon and shrimp, early, before the rush comes."

Michael took a few gulps from his afternoon tea, "What are we doing for dinner, tonight? What do you say we just take it easy, order a family size pizza and relax?"

Everyone thought that was a great idea.

And that was the last time tea was had with Linsey in the afternoon. And it was the last evening spent with her Earthly husband who sat, cuddled, next to his questionable lover. Surely Michael would eventually learn of the danger that Amber presented to the family. But would it be too late?

On her final night in the Dickly castle, wine was not had with Linsey. After stuffing themselves with pizza, Michael and Amber only wished to sit before the TV in a drowsy state while contemplating going to sleep for the evening. Cuddled so close and warm, the two eventually fell asleep together, her head rested against his shoulder while his cheek rested against her head.

Then Michael stirred awake from a dream which pulled Amber from sleep as well.

Michael announced, "Well, I suppose we should call it a night."

Very groggy, Amber wished to dream some more with the man she loved. She softly made mention, "I feel so comfortable in your arms, like I could get the best night's sleep, ever."

Michael slowly rubbed her shoulder and arm with a look of promise that said, "Not tonight, but soon." Hopefully she would understand. For one, final night; the bed belonged to Linsey.

It was the last night Linsey would sleep with her Earthly husband. Michael turned to face her before switching off the light. "I'll always love you…" tears welled in his eyes. "Now I understand why you didn't want me to make a death mask of you. If I followed your wish, I would have been forced to say goodbye at the funeral. Instead, you have been with me since that day and watching over the family. You've been guiding Amber since she moved into this house. I know; she's still a young woman. Please trust her; she's done so much for us since coming in our lives."

Tears rolled down Michael's cheeks before turning off the light. He held Linsey in his arms all night, dreaming of their many years together and the wonderful moments in love. Then he awoke in the predawn, about two hours before the rest of the house would start their day.

An early-morning kiss was given to Linsey's forehead. "You'll always be in my heart; I'll always love you. This isn't goodbye, just a little change so that things can be normal around here. There's a place where you and I can continue to talk and have our relationship. But not here; not in this bed…"

…In the bed where Amber would soon sleep? Would Amber lay her head on the very pillow where Linsey's once did? Would Michael draw near to the young woman in the cold of night and cuddle in the very marital bed that was shared with Linsey for so many years?

An hour later, Michael approached the guest bedroom and carefully opened the door. Under normal circumstance, one should politely knock before entering a guest room. But Amber was more than a guest. Amber was a lover and someone who would soon share the bed each night with Michael.

Michael lightly tapped Amber on the shoulder while whispering. "Amber? Amber, wake up."

She inhaled, "Hmm…?"

"Amber, it's still very early; but I have something to show you."

"What is it? What's wrong? Is it Paulette?"

"Shh… don't wake Trista. No, Paulette's fine and sleeping. There's something else that I want to show you. Can you get dressed and meet me downstairs? Bring a jacket with, too."

Five minutes later, Amber quietly walked down the stairs with a jacket in her arms. Michael stood at the bottom.

"What is it, Michael? What do you want to show me?"

"You'll see. Will Trista be sleeping for about another hour?"

"She doesn't stir awake until just after six o'clock. Even then, she sits in her crib for a while."

Michael led Amber to the basement; an impressive living area, fully carpeted and finished with elaborate furnishings and full bar. She had been down there many times and never recalled it being chilly. Why did Michael ask her to bring a jacket?

Then Michael opened the door to the large wine cellar. Amber had never been in this room, but was immediately impressed with the finished oak wine shelves that could have appeared in an upscale winery. In addition, the flooring was finished with dark mahogany. The walls appeared to be covered with decorative bricks that were colored to match the floor.

There must have been hundreds—easily a couple thousand—bottles of wine in that cellar. Needless to say they were all organized according to type, brand and year. But what would Michael have to show Amber in this room? Did he buy her a collection of special wine? Did he throw out Linsey's Pinot Noir? Amber looked at him slightly dumbfounded as if waiting for more.

"We'll press onward from here." said Michael. He paused for a moment, "Do you smell that; that mustiness in the air, almost like something damp?"

Amber looked around, "Yeah, come to think of it I do notice the smell."

Michael smiled then walked over to what appeared to be the doorway of a small closet. He opened it, and then flipped on an industrial-sized light switch. "Take a look!"

From what Amber could see, beyond the door was a steep declining hallway that was illuminated by industrial track lighting. The floor was finished with rubber tile, obviously to prevent slipping brought on by any dampness. The hallway looked to descend about fifty feet below the basement.

Michael grabbed a large flashlight at the side of the wall. "We need to follow safety when going down there. You see the lighting on the ceiling? Well it runs all the way down there and is the only light we have. If there's a power failure or the line becomes faulty, we're pretty much screwed. Always take a flashlight!"

Mention of these things had Amber a bit uneasy. Where was Michael taking her? What was down there? She had no choice but to follow the man she loved, and trust him in that moment.

Halfway down the descending hallway, the sound of gentle, trickling water could be heard. It wasn't until reaching the bottom of the hallway and turning left that Amber realized what was below the basement. Michael had a cave on his property!

"You have a cave?"

He was proud to inform her, "Not just a little cave; this actually spirals below the mountain to a network of deep caverns. I never had the place fully explored; never wanted people to know about it. The builder discovered it when this house was in construction. It's my mountain, my land and my cavern. I told him to make sure the basement has access to the cave and install electric lighting for me. But it only goes so far. Do you want to check it out?"

"Sure!" In all the vacations Amber's family had been on through the years, Amber never toured a cave. And it's a shame, really. As she would soon find out, caverns are one of the world's most beautiful places.

Hiking the path that was illuminated by mounted lights on various walls felt as though walking down a hill with gravity pulling the way. They were inside the mountain and descending towards the bottom which was nearly four-hundred feet.

After a couple minutes of walking, they reached a chamber. Michael stopped. "Let me know if you ever need a rest. I want to show you something that could be very helpful when navigating yourself in a cave to prevent getting lost. I'm sure you've looked up at white, puffy clouds and recognized the shapes of animals and peoples' faces, right? Down here, the same can be done. If you allow your imagination to do so, many of the grottos and rock formations take on recognizable shapes." Michael pointed the flashlight at an area in the chamber. "Do you see a Christmas tree?"

Amber immediately noticed the shape, "Oh, yeah!"

"That's why I call this the Christmas tree chamber. It's just one of a few chambers that run through these caverns. Each one is named after a rock formation or grotto. Based on the chambers and various recognizable shapes, you can determine where you are in the cavern."

Michael continued to walk, "Come on; let me show you more." As they ventured further down, Amber couldn't help but be impressed with the dramatic breaks in ceilings which revealed a hundred feet above. Occasionally, water would drop on her face. Michael laughed as she wiped the droplet off in annoyance. "Those drops of water are good luck! Look above!" Michael shined the flashlight at the lower portion of the ceiling. "See the stalactites? Sometimes water from a stalactite will drop on you. This is called a cave-kiss and is considered good luck."

"I've got a few kisses from the cave already. It must be my lucky day." said Amber.

Occasionally, Michael and Amber would pass a gentle stream or small pool of water. Water seemed to be the running symphony throughout the cavern. At some point, Michael let her know that the water was 99% pure, and fit for drinking. Filtering through soil and clay for thousands of years, the water had been purified.

After about twenty minutes of downward hiking and passing four chambers, Michael announced, "We are now reaching the bottom of the mountain and the final chamber that I want to show you." He paused at a nearly-arched entryway that appeared to be lit by candlelight. "This is Linsey's chamber." He carefully entered the room with Amber behind. And directly in the center where a medium-sized grotto stood was Linsey's statue-head, seated on top. Surrounding the grotto were several large candles that were supported by tall fixtures staked into the ground. The chamber looked to be some sort of church altar with Linsey being the god.

Linsey stared at Amber from the grotto, appearing to be very unhappy with the new arrangement. But for Amber, it was the perfect place for the relic. Finally, Amber could enjoy her days in the Dickly castle without any interference from Linsey. Four-hundred feet below was the perfect place. And Linsey had her own chamber!

Soon, Amber speculated the possibility of finally sleeping with Michael. But she wasn't going to say anything at the moment. Instead, she commented on the lit candles. "Will the burning candles use up any oxygen down here?"

Michael laughed, "Of course not! There's plenty of air down here! And if you've noticed, throughout the caverns, there are natural chimneys that provide plenty of circulation."

Amber didn't know what to say. Really she was ecstatic to have the object that tormented her day and night to finally be out of the home. "Well it's beautiful, Michael. And Linsey looks to be so happy to have her own chamber."

Amber was lying, of course! Anyone looking at Linsey at that moment would certainly notice the face of resentment and outrage.

Even Michael lied in agreement, "She certainly does look happy. And she's such a beautiful woman." Secretly he would have rather taken Linsey back upstairs and lay her head on the pillow in bed. And Michael wouldn't dare make mention of the gift that would be given to Amber later that night!

* * *

'Twas the night before Christmas; Paulette and Trista slept soundly while Michael and Amber sat in their usual cuddle spot on the sofa. Christmas Eve was definitely a special celebration for the family. Four o'clock mass was attended and featured a small production of the nativity, performed by a group of children in the church. Afterwards, the family returned home and enjoyed Paulette's favorite meal served each year of cold, smoked salmon and shrimp cocktail. And now she slept in bed, possibly dreaming of her romantic boyfriend who lived so, far away.

This was the first night when Amber was finally able to enjoy the man she loved without the jealous wife glaring from the distance. Suddenly, Michael presented Amber a gift; a small, wrapped box that would have been a bit large and heavy for jewelry. Judging by the size and weight, Amber assumed it to be perfume.

"It's only a little something to open before Christmas morning. It's nothing big. Go ahead, open it!" said Michael. Every year Michael presented Linsey a small gift on Christmas Eve, and intended to continue the tradition with Amber. He wouldn't tell her this, of course.

It was a bottle of Opium, the recognizable Oriental-spiced perfume that some might consider to be an unusual gift for a young woman. Michael always loved the smell of Opium. Its warm scent brought about a subliminal framework of a sexy red for him.

Amber didn't find the perfume to be unusual. It came from the man she loved and looked to be expensive. She sprayed a tiny amount on her wrist and took a deep inhale. "Mmmmmm… I can't wait to try it."

Michael held Amber's wrist up and took a whiff for himself, "Mmmmmm… it smells good on you. I could just eat you up right now!" Soon he combed his fingers behind her hair and gave a passionate kiss. Is this the effect that Opium has on a man? Maybe it was limited to Michael. Amber would be sure to spray some on for Christmas morning.

Michael pulled away from the kiss. "Well, I suppose we should get to bed so Santa Clause can come."

Amber wasn't going to say a word. Words were not necessary. She knew where bed was for that night and the nights to follow. She humbly entered the enormous master bedroom, and slipped under the covers with Michael. There wasn't time to get sleepwear in her old bedroom, and it wasn't necessary! 'Twas the night before Christmas and Amber would sleep naked on Linsey's side of the bed with the subtle hint of Opium on her wrist and Michael's naked, warm body huddled close. It was the best night of sleep she had gotten in her entire life!

Chapter Sixteen

What better gift for Amber than to wake up Christmas morning in Michael's arms?

"Good morning…" said Amber with a bright smile on her face.

"Good morning…" Michael kissed his beautiful Amber on the forehead. "And Merry Christmas!"

Michael did his usual routine of venturing downstairs into the kitchen to brew coffee. Amber's routine was slightly different than in previous mornings as she would now peak into Trista's bedroom to check if her daughter was sleeping. With the child in dreamland, Amber decided to get a jump start on Paulette, who was already awake and eager for her daily email from Todd. But this was Christmas morning, a time to open presents and enjoy whatever special breakfast Amber was going to make for the holiday. Such are the grueling moments that a young lady must endure when in love. She would have liked nothing more than for Todd to be by her side, wishing her a Merry Christmas and offering wonderful presents that were a testament of his love.

The Dickly family always has Christmas breakfast before even thinking of opening presents under the tree. And un-like other mornings, before making breakfast, Amber wished to ready herself for the day—shower, groom, dress and spray on some more of that sexy Opium that seemed to drive Michael wild on the night before Christmas. Of course these things were all done in the oversized master bathroom that she now shared with Michael.

While waiting for Amber, Paulette and Father sat in the kitchen, enjoying their morning cups of coffee together. Father had no idea that his princess drank coffee. "Did Amber introduce you to coffee?"

Paulette nodded.

"Yeah, she's definitely a wonderful person. What do you think? Does she have your approval?"

Paulette nodded with the straw in her mouth while taking another sip from the cup.

Amber finally entered the kitchen, all dolled up for Christmas morning with a generous spray of her Opium perfume.

Suddenly, Paulette hated Amber with all her heart. Only moments ago she agreed with Father that Amber was a wonderful person. How she wished she could have taken it back. It was bad enough that Amber wore her hair like Mother's, dyed it to resemble her color; not to mention quickly moved in to be Father's new lover and most-likely future bride. But this new stunt was by-far the dirtiest. The sense of smell is most powerful and activates memories so powerful and strong. How dare Amber wear Mother's perfume? It felt as-if Mother now went about the kitchen on Christmas morning.

Paulette only looked at Amber with a sad expression that asked, "Why? Why are you doing this to me?"

Thankfully, Paulette had a special friend to confide in. She would certainly tell Todd of this! In her yearning for Todd to be near, she kept mental notes of all the occurrences of Christmas morning to share with him. Aside from Amber wearing Mother's perfume, Paulette had to endure eating the so-called Christmas omelet that included mushrooms. Paulette hated mushrooms!

She would certainly make mention of all the wonderful jewelry and clothes that Father gave to Amber. And how she would love to mention sitting in the wheelchair while people opened gifts before her. New CDs, a new CD player, some books, a few videos and some more clothes for her winter wardrobe: Christmas didn't have the excitement as in earlier years when Paulette was able to touch the presents. But this thought would remain a secret from Todd, for he was yet to be aware of Paulette's physical condition. Many times she wished to reveal this, but feared it might have been too early. Some day he would know; and some day he would be with her in person, maybe even take her as his bride and carry her over the threshold into his home.

* * *

Throughout the holidays and early January, Michael noticed a change in his daughter. "Where's Paulette?" he asked several times in those days.

To which Amber would always answer, "Upstairs in her room."

To Michael, this brought to mind the recent images of his daughter facing the keyboard and monitor with a pencil in her mouth. She had gotten highly skilled with typing and resembled a woodpecker that tapped away at the keys. Michael supposed it was normal for a teenage girl to isolate herself from the family. But beyond that speculation, he had no idea of the new reality provided by the computer.

Had Father cared to take a closer look, he would have discovered that a stranger managed to create an elaborate reality, bridging the many miles between himself and Paulette. Todd was more than an electrical engineer who worked for a robotics development company. Todd had a natural, God-given talent for writing. With this gift, he wished more than to simply titillate the recipient living hundreds of miles away. He wished to mesmerize Paulette with tales of fantastic places that he and she traveled to. He wished to stir powerful emotions in Paulette and lead her to develop a longing for him. The stories of Todd and Paulette had the power to draw her deeper into a personal realm of fantasy. To make matters worse, she contributed to the stories so that they shared a private world together.

"Where is one place you've always wanted to go?" asked Todd in an email.

"Before my mother got sick, she always promised that we would go to Paris one day—just her and I."

And so Todd was sure to book a flight to Paris for a romantic getaway with Paulette in May. This was all done in fantasy, of course. They strolled the shops, cafes and cinemas along the Avenue des Champs-Élysées. They were sure to visit the Arc de Triomphe and took the stairway to the top for a view of the surrounding avenues. Without a care in the world and no obligations but to enjoy one another's company, they would stay in Paris until the early evening. Some nights that would enjoy an evening tour and dinner in Paris before escaping on a train back to their country guesthouse where they drank champagne and wine while making beautiful love into the late evening hours. The described lovemaking could have easily been an erotic tale in itself. Imagine the feelings, emotions and chemistry that pounded through the young girl's heart while reading this!

Todd took Paulette on many other romantic getaways. Tours of London followed by a stay in the English country to visit old castles was had through fantasy.

They enjoyed lazy, tropical resorts with nothing to do but drink all afternoon and make love on the beach before retiring to bed for the evening. And they were sure to sleep in until around lunch, when their busy day of relaxation would begin.

When romantic getaways were becoming a stale subject, Todd began to create suspenseful tales of him and Paulette. Both were dangerously involved in espionage and could not be together because of international tensions. But they wanted each other, loved each other so badly! With opposing enemy spies on both sides hunting for them, Todd and Paulette enjoyed secret and dangerous rendezvous' when they would viciously attack one another under the heat of international intrigue.

And then there were the trashy tales of Paulette being a sexy criminal who was taken to the station late at night for questioning. It wasn't necessary to handcuff the suspect to the chair, but Todd took great pleasure in doing this. And while alone with Paulette in the interrogation room, would the lead detective actually lose his morals and strip the suspect for "dirty" interrogation tactics? Paulette learned just how much of a dirty cop Todd was!

Of course, in between all the stories and fantasies, Todd and Paulette wrote of their normal lives. And Todd was beginning to mention of how easy it would be to book a flight to finally meet Paulette. The two were definitely falling in love and needed to encounter one another in person.

Paulette wondered what sort of life she would have with Todd, considering her physical condition. He proved through all the stories and fantasies that through imagination and a little work they could enjoy a beautiful love together. Paulette believed that when finally married, Todd would care for her in the same way that Mother and Amber did. And her strongest wish was most simple: to truly feel Todd's kiss on her lips while he warmly embraced her. The time had finally come. Todd's true love would be tested by learning of Paulette's physical condition.

* * *

It was late January, and Father was only a day's return from a business trip. It was on this day when Paulette pecked out a serious email in response to finally meeting Todd in person.

She told him everything; the bicycle accident and how it damaged the area of her brain for speech while leaving her paralyzed from the neck, down. She confessed to communicating to him through "pecking" out sentences on the keyboard. And Paulette reminded him of how much in love she was while mentioning that love knows no obstacles. A little work and imagination could go far if Todd was willing to overlook the flaws.

For Todd; online, long-distance dating was done for a very, good reason. He may have seemed like a fantastic guy behind the emails; but in the real world, women had difficulty taking any relationship with him beyond an initial date or two. True, Todd was a good-looking guy who made money. But Amber's initial impressions of Paulette's boyfriend were surprisingly accurate—as disappointing as that may be to the reader.

In recent years, Todd had gone through an awakening—sort of a rebirth that young men experience after a couple decades of being treated disrespectfully. Todd had gone through high school and college with the reputation as a wimpy, puny, dweeby sort of guy; a nerd, if you will. And although landing a successful career shortly after college, he found that coworkers and higher-ups had little or no respect for him.

Throughout his life, Todd had a dream to study martial arts, believing it would unlock his ability to transform into something greater. With nothing more to do with his life than work the nine-to-five, Todd decided to sign up for a martial arts class. He diligently trained while earning one belt after another. Eventually he developed a mindset of confidence which soon led to the belief that he could transform himself into whatever he liked.

Why should Todd have had a puny, skinny body? He joined a weightlifting gym and toned his pectorals, biceps and deltoids. Then he signed up for man camp and was taught to walk like he had something between his legs.

Todd spent much time looking at magazines with images of ripped steroid monkeys and then staring at himself in the mirror to compare. He was almost there… in his own mind. Although toned with slight muscle development, there was nothing spectacular of his physique. But he spoke with a newly-acquired, jocular voice and walked with an overly-confident gait. He obtained a motorcycle license and cruised the open highways in his ninja-style crotch rocket. With this exaggerated, self-perception of greatness; Todd reached a peak state of physical, mental and spiritual being. And it was finally time for Todd to find a woman.

It wouldn't have been too difficult for Todd to find a woman, had he come down to Earth and been himself. And maybe some dating etiquette would have been a wise investment. There was a little problem with Todd. Behind his good looks, toned body, jocular voice, confident air and lots of money; Todd was nothing more than a self-worshipping, arrogant nerd who prided himself in knowing everything about everything. He had no problem finding dates with women, but in the course of the first twenty minutes of a date, Todd would take the initial conversation piece and provide a detailed text book explanation of what he understood. Take for example; if exercise was mentioned, Todd would provide a graduate-course lecture on human physiology. If his date mentioned car trouble from the previous day, Todd would provide an entire physics discussion on combustion engines—every gear, every piston and every stroke that would lead to thermal viscosity breakdown. After twenty minutes, Todd's date would feel as though she had popped in an audio lecture cassette and was soon falling asleep. Rarely was a woman able to speak during a date with Todd, as he did all the talking. And behind the emulated manliness that failed to drip true testosterone, the woman seated across the table would soon think to herself, "Oh my gosh! This guy is a total geek!"

And it was worse than that! Todd had a certain degree of immaturity in his interactions with people. Now self-perceived as a demigod, the world was all about Todd and his needs. He had no empathy or consideration for the people around him. Thanks to overly-developed self-confidence, and his quest to rightfully take back what the world had stolen in younger years, all that mattered to Todd was his own feelings. Where as you and I reach a point in our lives when we temporarily deny our own emotional needs, sometimes accept not-so desirable situations for the sake of maintaining peace and harmony with a larger picture; Todd was quick to strike down anything that wasn't in his best interest.

It was all about Todd. He would never settle for second best. He read Paulette's email and replied.

"Paulette,

Your email has come as quite a surprise for me. I sat in the chair for nearly an hour and tried to draw a single, recognizable emotion. There were just so many of them.

I guess I should start off by saying that I'm very hurt. (*It was all about Todd's feelings!*) I feel as though you had been lying to me all along. And I'm sad to know that I lived a lie all these weeks. Let me tell you; had I flown out there to discover you in a wheelchair, paralyzed and unable to speak, I would have been very angry. In fact, I would have had a difficult time dealing with my anger and other hurt emotions. It's a good thing you told me this now!

Did you really think that you could have a relationship with someone like me? After all that I've learned in life, I know that I deserve so much more. I'm sorry, but I can't see something like that working. I mean don't they have a dating service for handicapped people?

Glad you finally told the truth, and have a nice life..."

He didn't bother to sign the email, much less provide a proper goodbye. Poor Paulette read the shocking reply while feeling all her hopes, dreams and love she experienced in those weeks drain from her body. Physically, she wished to react to the disturbing news; but was unable to move, thanks to her condition. Instead, shock and adrenaline surged through her veins. Her heart raced like those nights under the sheets with Todd's imagined presence. But instead of pleasure, there was a crushing pain near the heart and abdomen. No one ever prepared Paulette for a time when all her hopes and dreams in love would be shattered to pieces. Poor Paulette had no idea what was happening to her. She was experiencing a broken heart.

There was nothing unusual of Paulette to sit motionless in her wheelchair as she was paralyzed from the neck, down. But her eyes were always alive. Her face displayed a large range of expressions and she had the notable pink coloring of Mother's face. Paulette often turned her head to observe her surroundings. But for two hours after reading Todd's cruel email, Paulette sat motionless in a catatonic state with a pale, lifeless face.

Just before lunch, Amber finally entered Paulette's room. Only two hours ago, she dialed online so the girl could check email in privacy. In just two hours, Paulette transformed into a lifeless shell with expressionless face.

"Paulette?" Amber placed her hand on the paralyzed girl to ensure that all was well. She was breathing and had body temperature. But something was terribly wrong. "Paulette, are you okay?"

Paulette didn't bother to look up or answer Amber.

"Oh my gosh; Paulette, what's wrong with you?" Did she receive bad news in one of Todd's emails? Checking the screen was the only natural thing to do. Amber read the cruel email that was displayed on the monitor. "You told him about your condition?"

A tear could be seen running down Paulette's cheek as her lips quivered. Then she sniffled.

Amber was nearly in tears, herself, upon seeing the young girl destroyed. She embraced Paulette, "Oh, Honey; I'm so sorry. I know you're hurt by this. Guys are such jerks, I know. You'll pull through this." Then she gently released her embrace while rubbing Paulette's shoulder. "Do you know what you need in a moment like this? You need to be with someone. You can't sit up here alone in a depression."

Amber logged off the Internet and shut down the computer. "That's enough for now! You've been sitting before this thing for too many weeks and I was beginning to think maybe it wasn't good for you." Then she took hold of the wheelchair and spun Paulette towards the door. "Downstairs you go. We're going to have lunch, brew a pot of coffee and just talk about guys for the afternoon—see if we can't pull you through this. I know it hurts. But you have to move on."

Amber realized that food was probably the least thing on Paulette's mind. "I made you half a sandwich and a cup of soup. If you can just eat a little and then we'll hang out in the family room for the day. I was starting to miss you. For weeks you've been upstairs typing away."

After lunch, Amber brewed a pot of coffee and wheeled Paulette into the living room. As seen outside the front window, it was a cold and cloudy day in January with snow on the ground; perfect for recovering from a broken heart and just talking out feelings.

But Amber did most of the talking that afternoon. She told the story of the first boy who had broken her heart. She spoke of the many guys who had hurt her and how she learned to pick up the pieces and move on. "You've never dated before so this is all so, very new to you. Love has been known to hurt, and it most-often does. But you'll be alright. By tomorrow when your Father comes home, you'll forget about Todd and this will all be behind you." In no way could Paulette be in this condition when Michael came home!

Amber's talking did have a positive effect on Paulette. She began to suspect that perhaps there was some truth to what Amber was saying. Perhaps everyone experiences a broken heart.

But in the evening after being tucked into bed with the lights turned out, Todd's imagined presence was not to found. For so many nights the tops of the blankets were his strong arms that held Paulette. He would whisper, "I love you" and all sorts of sweet nothings into her ear. For so many nights he kissed her lips and made love to Paulette until she fell asleep. But tonight the bed was cold.

Then, like a flood of light, hope filled the young girl's heart. Maybe Todd thought things over and regretted his cruel words. Perhaps he already emailed her with a lengthy letter of apology. "Please forgive me! Please come back to me!"

So much in love, Paulette would certainly forgive him. How she wanted so badly to check email, but her blasted physical condition made it impossible. She would have to wait until morning when Amber logged in and opened the email of apology. For now, Paulette could only close her eyes and send messages of telepathy to her lover, "You hurt me, today. You have no idea what you did to me. But I forgive you. I love you so much! Please believe me that we can make this work. My condition is only an obstacle that love can easily conquer."

Then she softly cried while continuing to send her telepathic messages, "I want you to hold me like you've done every night."

Finally, Todd's warm arms lay across Paulette. She fell asleep, occasionally awakening to feel if he was still there.

Chapter Seventeen

It was the following morning, and Michael was to return home from his business trip some time before lunch.

Being that Amber now slept in the master bedroom and Trista in her own room, the alarm clock was only heard by Amber. This meant that Trista was no longer awoken by the alarm, provided she wasn't already awake. Some mornings, she eagerly bounced in her crib. Other mornings she remained sleeping, which gave Amber a jump start on Paulette. Trista remained sleeping on the morning after Paulette's traumatic breakup.

Much to Amber's surprise, the new day offered a flood of hope and a near light that shined through Paulette's bedroom door when opened.

"Good morning! You look like you're in a better mood today."

Paulette nodded. Then she looked over to the computer.

"What? You want me to wheel the computer over? Don't you want to go to the bathroom first?"

Again, Paulette motioned her face towards the computer.

Seeing that Paulette had something important to say, Amber wheeled the cart over and supported the paralyzed girl upright to peck away at the keyboard with pencil in her mouth.

Paulette pecked a simple sentence, "Login to my email."

This was not good! Only hours from Michael returning home, Paulette managed to elevate her mood with a false belief that

Todd had a change of heart. "Honey, why would you want to do that? You're only going to throw yourself back to the beginning."

"Login to my email!" Paulette demanded.

"Alright, fine! You want to see if maybe Todd has thought things over and is crawling back to you? I'll login, but you have to promise me something. You have to be realistic. Chances are there isn't an email from Todd. And if you don't see an email, I don't want you to fall apart. Can you promise me that?"

Paulette only beamed from ear-to-ear as if she received some overpowering premonition that promised there to be an email from Todd.

What was Amber to do in this situation? Paulette was blind with hope and didn't hear a word from Amber. Perhaps if Amber stalled some, in hopes for Paulette to return to Earth. She suggested, "Don't you want to use the bathroom first?"

Paulette shook her head, no.

Amber reluctantly dialed online and listened to the annoying scream of the modem. She clicked the email icon, and was sure to do everything in front of Paulette's hopeful face. But much to Paulette's dismay, there were no new messages.

"See, Honey; I told you. You shouldn't bring your hopes up like that." Amber wheeled the crane device over to the bed and connected it to Paulette. "Maybe in about a week we'll check it again, see if there's anything. And you know, just because he apologizes with an email, doesn't mean you should immediately forgive him and come back to him. He's a jerk for what he said to you. If he does send you an email of apology, let him sit for about a week and suffer in his own doing."

Paulette went through her usual morning activities while being supported by the crane device. While suspended midair and waiting for the bathtub to fill, her expression of grief returned. The previous night was all fantasy. Todd's warm arms were simply imagined. The telepathic communication was nothing more than hopeful words thought in the darkness. Todd was nowhere, and he meant every word of cruelty in his final email. He was gone forever. If only Paulette could have turned back the clock, the morning might have been different and most likely brought with it a loving email from Todd.

With the tub finally filled, Paulette was lowered into the water. Immediately, Amber gently poured the bucket of water over Paulette's hair. Although Paulette was supported upright with head slightly tilted back, drops of water ran down her face. It didn't take Amber long to realize that these were tears.

Amber sighed. This was going to be a long and difficult day. If only she had another twenty-four hours before Michael's return, Paulette would surely recover from the heartbreak. What condition would Paulette be in later this morning when her father returned? Would there be more crying? How would Amber explain?

Amber thought of a few scenarios. "She's just happy for your return, Michael. I've noticed that your weeklong absences affect her." That would only make matters worse. Amber would be lying and appearing to cover something important from Michael. Perhaps if she hinted to the truth, "I guess she was talking to some guy online and he kind of broke up with her. She's heartbroken…" Although closer to the truth, the explanation would still attempt to cover the whole truth. Exactly how was Paulette able to talk to some guy online? Where would Paulette have gotten the idea to do such a thing? Amber was to care for and protect Paulette, act out the role of mother in her life. Despite the trust she had gained from Michael, and the new levels reached in love, Amber failed Michael. Paulette was in this sad condition because of Amber. It was all Amber's fault. Amber hadn't fully cared for Paulette.

More tears streamed from Paulette's face. It brought Amber to her rope's end. Panic-stricken she brought her face near to Paulette's. There was a tone of urgency, almost near shouting in Amber's voice. "Paulette, listen to me! You have to pull yourself together! You can't let yourself fall apart over this!" Amber was in serious trouble! There was no way to reconstruct the shattered girl!

Paulette sniffled to be followed by a cry and heavy weeping. Tears, snot and drool ran along her face; her lifeless body adding to the appearance of one who had lost complete control of body and mind. It would become one of the most frightening moments of Amber's life as no one prepared her to care for a young, paralyzed girl who had spiraled into a mental breakdown.

Amber didn't understand the flood of emotions experienced by Paulette. The many weeks of dreamy love suddenly disappeared. All those nights of lying next to Todd as he whispered sweet nothings in her ear were all fantasy. And what was reality, now? Was it any better than the place she was in?

Paulette continued to weep throughout her bath, while being dried off with the towel and while having her hair blow dried. How much longer would this go on?

Finally, Amber broke her own silence and called out, "Paulette? Paulette?"

There was no answer from the scrunched up, teary-eyed, sobbing face.

Amber screamed in a shrilling voice while shaking the girl, "Paulette, stop it!" Then Amber provided a slap to Paulette's cheek, exactly the way her own mother often did. It shocked Paulette and provided a moment of deep regret for Amber as she immediately embraced the girl and cried out, "I'm sorry... Oh my gosh, I'm sorry! I don't know what else to do! You promised me! You promised you would keep this a secret from your father. I can't have you in this condition."

No one ever slapped Paulette before and it came as quite a surprise. In addition, she appeared to understand Amber's concern and did calm down some.

Amber lightly stroked Paulette's hair, "Now I've been through this and I understand your pain. But you have to trust me."

Paulette nodded.

* * *

At 11:30, precisely, the musical horn of the limousine sounded as it approached the Dickly castle. Michael was home and eager to see his sorely missed family.

Amber greeted her man with open, loving arms; nearly providing a look of reassurance that all was well.

Paulette, too, was anxious to see Father. Her eyes glassed as he entered the family room and approached the wheelchair. How she longed for Mother at such a delicate time in her life. Father was the next best thing to Mother, but no one would understand. Perhaps this is why she fell into another fit of crying.

Michael was surprised, "What? What is it, Honey?"

Like a downpour that follows a gentle rain, her cries turned into heavy weeping.

Michael turned to Amber. "What's wrong with her?"

Amber's face froze, not sure of what to say.

Michael's voice increased, "What did you do her? Why is she like this?"

Amber shook her head and began to cry, herself. "I'm sorry… I'm sorry! I didn't mean it, Michael! You have to believe me!"

Michael nearly growled, "What? What did you do to her?"

How could Amber explain the complexity? All she could do was signal Michael to follow while continuing to apologize. Paulette remained weeping. And little Trista joined in the choir of crying as she could sense the intense emotions of the moment. She toddled behind Michael and Mother and cried all the louder upon seeing Mommy run up the stairs without her.

Paulette's computer remained logged into her email account. Amber opened the final email from Todd and informed Michael, "She had a boyfriend online. He found out about her condition and broke up with her."

Keep in mind this was the mid-90s. Very, few people in those times heard of online romances. Mention of Paulette's boyfriend had Michael confused. "Boyfriend?" He leaned over to read the cruel email, after which he demanded, "What else was he sending her?"

Amber had no choice but to be helpful at the moment. She showed Michael how to close an email and view the previously read messages of the inbox.

Confident he understood how to view his daughter's mailbox, he ordered, "Look out!" It was the first time Michael had ever spoken harshly to Amber. Then he pulled the computer cart over to the bedside and sat down.

For over two hours Michael carefully read every email between his daughter and some strange man living hundreds of miles away. Every story, every fantasy and every empty promise was finally read by Father. For weeks he would walk past Paulette's room and see her pecking away at the keyboard. Today we are aware of strangers online who talk to our children. But for Michael, he would have never imagined that such a thing was possible. While reading the shocking emails, he had to wonder if there were laws against a grown man interacting with a minor so provocatively.

Unsure of how to react, Michael stormed out of his daughter's bedroom, into his office and slammed the door shut.

All afternoon he remained in his office until emerging for a brief moment to silently venture down the stairs and into the kitchen for a sandwich and drink. He didn't bother to look into the family room where Amber sadly sat with Paulette. Then again, Amber wouldn't have known of this for her eyes remained fixed to the floor in deep shame.

It was mostly, if not all, her fault for what happened to Paulette. Amber understood this. And she certainly wasn't going to be angry with Paulette, for the girl was only acting out her natural feelings. If there was anyone outside of Amber to be angry with, it would have been Todd. And the more Amber thought of his name, his profile picture and his exaggerated self-perception of himself; the more furious Amber became.

It was Friday afternoon, and surely he would go for a nice cruise on his ninja-style crotch rocket after work. Maybe he even took his motorcycle to work in the morning. Such is the luxury when living in an area of warmer temperatures.

How dare he treat a paralyzed girl this way? How dare he spend weeks building up her hopes and causing her to fall in love? And when she finally felt it best to disclose her limiting condition, Todd refused to display any empathy on his part. It only proved to Amber that some people need to experience a tragic misfortune to understand the pain and suffering of others.

Motorcycles can be dangerous, especially when driven by carefree, heartless individuals who lack any empathy or under-standing of others. This doesn't mean to say that motorcycle accidents only happen to bad people. Remember, this was Am-ber's world and her own emotionally-driven thoughts. There are plenty of unfortunate souls who experience an undeserving ac-cident on a bike. The same can be said of kind and wonderful people who may have experienced serious burns from the bar-beque, serious sprains of the ankle or nearly-fatal car crashes. It's just that sometimes these terrible things need to happen to bad people as well (in Amber's mind).

Amber sat motionless in her pool of negative emotions. She dwelled on every bit of shame and projected it outwards to some imagined cloud. With it was mixed her rage towards Todd and the sadness felt for letting Linsey down. Amber would fix this and make it up to Linsey. And in doing so, maybe she would regain her trust from Michael.

In the imagined cloud of emotions was injected a terrible fan-tasy of some life-changing accident that was truly deserved, and might lead to the development of empathy and understanding of those less fortunate. And if you've come to know Amber, then you know that these emotionally-driven fantasies hatch into reality.

Hundreds of miles away, a trucker pulled over to a highway oasis for fuel. We like to think that every safety protocol is observed when working with dangerous machines that carry, on average, one-hundred gallons of fuel. But who is to say that a trucker would never become distracted while fueling up and accidentally leave the gas cap off the tank?

And who is to say that he wouldn't neglect to take notice of the missing cap upon returning to the truck after paying for the fuel? The trucker shifted through all his gears while slowly traveling the entrance ramp to the open highway. It was Friday afternoon in a rural setting with only an occasional commuter that traveled home.

For nearly two miles the trucker traveled the open highway while gallons of diesel fuel sprayed along the road. It wasn't until one of those far-and-few-between commuters spotted the semi truck with leaky fuel, that the trucker was signaled to indicate a problem. The trucker waved a thank you at the helpful motorist, pulled over to the shoulder and immediately realized that the gas cap was left at the oasis. Fortunately he had a spare in his toolbox for a mishap like this. It was best to replace the cap and head back on the road before a state trooper noticed any spill. Diesel spills, as you may know, are a terrible hazard to motorists. Not only is diesel combustible, but it can be present a serious slip hazard, leading to accidents.

This was the same highway that Todd commuted home each day. And on this particular Friday, he did, in fact, ride his ninja-style crotch rocket to the office. Stepping out into the parking lot on a fine, Friday afternoon; Todd was in his usual exaggerated state of peak physical, mental and spiritual greatness. He was a great man with a mind of vast intellect, and built like a god. From inside the office, a coworker may have watched Todd and secretly thought, "I'm so sick of that crap! Why doesn't he just give it up?"

Of course Todd was sure to wear a helmet for safety with a tinted visor. As far as protection from road rash, he was going to have to live dangerously. A leather wouldn't have protected him from what was about to happen anyway!

Zooming along the highway with an engine that sounded like a high-tech wash machine winding on second gear, Todd was master of his own destiny. But the fool he was, he didn't realize that it was now Amber's world. Where-as Todd was able to bridge hundreds of miles through titillating fantasies that eventually destroyed a young girl; Amber had the power to simply reach her hand across the void and affect any outcome desired.

Observing Amber that afternoon was the first time that Paulette felt a chilling fear of the woman. She watched as Amber sat in a near-death trance with the most fearsome and wicked look. Paulette had never been exposed to things metaphysical, but she could sense an undetectable noise radiating from Amber along with an invisible charge of energy. To Paulette, the family room was about to explode. She nearly cried out in hopes that Father would hear. But she remained silent, struggling to understand what was actually being seen and heard.

Hundreds of miles away, Todd carefully approached a utility van that traveled in the right lane. He wouldn't have any problem passing it up. Not more than a car lane ahead of the van, Todd lowered gears and accelerated to gain a thrilling velocity. This was done at a large splash of diesel fuel that had been left by the semi truck no more than fifteen minutes ago. At such a high speed, Todd lost control of the bike and soon found his own body slammed against the ground and rolling along the pavement. The driver of the utility van did everything in his power to avoid the bike and the unfortunate motorcyclist. The front and rear driver side tires ran over Todd's hips and thighs, seriously crushing and shattering bones. At least this stopped the excruciating scrapes along the pavement that was intensified by stinging diesel fuel to road rash. But it would be along time, if ever, before Todd could walk on his own two feet. Maybe now he would have an appreciation for being confined to a wheelchair.

Chapter Eighteen

It was about half-past midnight and just over twelve hours since the disaster unraveled at the Dickly castle. Very rarely do we hear of the woman being in the doghouse, but in this situation, Amber couldn't help but feel at fault. And she wasn't even going to try slipping in her own bed with Michael. Tonight, she opted to sleep in Trista's bedroom; awakening every forty-five minutes or so in such worry and apprehension. Surely her days—her hours—were numbered at the Dickly castle.

While lying on her side with eyes closed, Amber could hear the bedroom door carefully open and Michael enter. "Amber, are you sleeping?"

Amber immediately turned over to face him, "Not really…"

"Amber, why don't you come to bed? There's no reason for you to sleep in here. I'm still very angry and not sure how to react, but don't sleep in here tonight."

Through an afternoon and evening of giving the silent treatment, Michael was finally ready to speak to Amber. The punishment was clearly on his own terms; but again, Amber felt much at fault and was also disappointed in herself for failing the man she loved. Without saying a word, she stood up from bed, checked little Trista who slept in her crib and then cautiously walked out of the room and down the hall.

She sat on her side of the bed as Michael entered the room and closed the door. Michael softly spoke as if careful not to show anger. "Why, Amber? Why did you let this happen? How did this happen?"

"I'm sorry, Michael. It's just... We were talking about love and dating, and I realized she never had a boyfriend. I guess I thought... Well..."

Michael finished her statement, "Turning Paulette over to some stranger on the computer to talk dirty to her would make it all better? Amber, he didn't just talk dirty to her, he said all kinds of things and wrote all kinds of stories to make her fall in love. You don't know what it's like for someone in her condition. How do you know that words don't affect her differently than you and me?"

Amber sighed, "I didn't find an online pen pal for him to talk dirty to her. I just thought it would be nice for her to correspond with a friend, that's all. The sex talk came after all that."

"And you let it continue?"

"I didn't know how to stop her! I could see she was in love."

"Then you should have done like your mother and father would have done, and put a stop to it. You're supposed to be protecting her and taking care of her."

Up until recently, Amber would have argued that interfering with Paulette's love life would have made matters worse and resulted in a negative, long-term outcome. But seeing the results of the past twenty-four hours, she had grown into realizing that parents aren't supposed to be a teenager's friend. If only she understood this sooner.

"I'm sorry, Michael. I really am."

Still very angry, but wishing to restore peace in the house, Michael walked over to his side of the bed and slipped back under the covers. "I know you are. I can see that. Make sure you turn your light off before falling asleep."

It was such a halfhearted attempt of making up and show-ing forgiveness. But it was probably all for very, good reason. Amber failed Michael's test; a clear indicator that she was not up to the task of caring for Paulette in Michael's absence. Being that Amber placed Paulette in danger, she was the last person Michael should have trusted. But he loved Amber and needed her so badly. What was he to do? It was too late to fire the care-taker. Michael would fall to pieces upon seeing Amber pack up and leave the Dickly castle forever. As the days passed, he de-cided to never show forgiveness; only realize how sorry Amber was and see how she had grown from the experience. Perhaps this unhealed wound would have forced Amber to be more care-ful in the future.

But an unhealed and unaddressed transgression was easy for Amber to overlook, being that the early spring months brought conversations of marriage, soon to follow an actual proposal with enormous engagement ring and ultimately a beautiful wedding in June.

But you don't wish to be bothered with the boring details of a perfect wedding made possible by Michael Dickly's wealth. Rest assured it was everything Amber ever wished for. And it made possible for her to overlook those loose ends, mainly items on her own side of the family.

To begin with, Mother and Father refused to meet or acquaint themselves with their daughter's future husband. Already a few surgeries and still in casts from the accident, Mother was deathly frightened of Amber after that terribly cold day in De-cember. Father and Amber's own brother and sister were brain-washed by Mother. The family shared the belief that Amber was now the estranged member. Out of decency, they did attend the wedding and reception, but remained distant. And it wasn't un-til near the last minute when Father had a change of heart and decided to walk his daughter down the aisle. After all, what terrible crime did Amber commit? She fell in love with a wealthy man and would spend the rest of her life in comfort.

Way in the distance of that day, Amber noticed a subtle and frightening strangeness. Against what would have been Mother's wishes, Amber was sure to invite everyone on her side of the family. This included the outcasts of strange people who lived about an hour away from the Mapleview and Sillmac area. Throughout her life, Mother insisted on never associating with those people. One of these people was Mother's own sister.

Throughout the day of Amber's wedding, she could feel the strange people in the distance carefully watching her. They studied her while speaking in such a way that their whispered words could be heard by Amber—even from a distance.

But Amber ignored them, insisting that she was not one of them. Occasionally one of the strange people would approach and congratulate Amber with eyes deeply set into Amber's as if carefully reading and seeing through her. Of course she was sure to mask herself. Amber was a happy, young woman who married the man of her dreams. That was the only thing important on that day, and the mask she wore to fool everyone, including herself.

* * *

It is also worth mentioning the honeymoon that Amber chose. With children each of their own, Michael and Amber's honeymoon was more of a family vacation. Paulette certainly couldn't take care of herself, and it would not be possible for Amber to have her own mother care for Trista while gone.

It was an easy solution for Michael. A nice two week cruise would have provided plenty of fun and relaxation for the family.

But Amber wasn't so thrilled with the idea. "Michael, how many cruises did you and Linsey go on as a family?"

"Oh, plenty! We'd go on a cruise at least twice a year. If not, we would spend a week at some tropical resort."

Amber quickly replied, "So that Paulette could do nothing but sit and enjoy the scenery?"

Michael was at a loss of words. How could Amber have cruelly stated the obvious? Of course Paulette was taken into consideration for each family vacation! She was confined to a wheelchair, and a cruise was easy. Just set her out on the pool deck all day.

Amber then asked, "Has Paulette ever been to Disney World?"

"No…"

Caring for a paralyzed girl would take much work. But being Paulette's new mother, Amber felt the best gift would have been to give her teenage daughter a fun-filled vacation at Disney World. She would ensure that every attraction, every ride and every show would be enjoyable for Paulette, regardless of any inconvenience brought on by her condition. And Disney makes plenty of accommodations for handicapped individuals. There was no reason for Paulette not to visit.

Chapter Nineteen

How times change! Married at twenty-three years-old; seven years later made Amber a woman of thirty. And seven years certainly aged Michael so that his hair turned all gray. Being that his business continued to expand, there was an increasing demand for Michael's attention; so much, in fact, that his body changed into that of an overworked businessman who spent many hours traveling, living in hotels and eating things that would certainly alter his physique into that of being mushy, flabby and unappealing.

But these things didn't cause Amber to feel as though she married the wrong man. It was the fact that Michael spent so much time away from home on business. And when not on business, most certainly he would be on golf outings with friends and colleagues, many of these outings in another state. Although pleasure, Michael stressed the importance of playing golf as it was his way of networking.

The beautiful, wilderness town of Sillmac has many of these stories of lonely housewives. With such an elite population of wealthy people, surely one spouse out of every marriage is overworked from a career. And this is why Amber did not blame herself for her recent behavior. A simple trip to the grocery store would usually precede stretching into a nice pair of tight-ass jeans and a matching top that boasted her beautiful skin. Sometimes her top would be low cut to reveal cleavage that had been squashed together by a pushup bra. Her hair would be done extra nice along with subtle hints of makeup that might have called out for attention. Amber was a lonely woman; and although not ready to surrender to infidelity, she needed to know that men still found her attractive.

Looking outstanding was important to Amber. Not all the women in the grocery store would be lonely housewives seeking attention. Some of them were quite happy in their marriages. It's just that times have changed, and married women remain attractive through the years.

There was once-upon-a-time when a wife might have walked past her husband who sat on the sofa, drinking a beer. The husband would be quick to ask, "Where are you going?"

"To the store."

"Dressed like that? I don't think so! Get back in the bedroom and put something decent on. You're not going out dressed like that!" And then he would take it a step further. "What are you getting at the store, anyway?"

"Milk... We need milk."

The husband would reassure his wife, "I've got enough for cereal in the morning. You don't need to run out and get milk. Stay home!"

And that would be the end of the conversation as any obedient wife would do as her husband said.

But today's husbands are so adoring and respectful of their wives. They realize there is cost for having an exceptionally beautiful wife and allow them to prance through the stores and public places with tight-ass jeans, revealing tops, done-up faces and styled hair. It's why my own wife won't even let me out of the house. There is plenty of heart-racing eye-candy walking the streets and shopping centers in my neighborhood.

Satisfied that she could compete with the other beautiful women who would be shopping that fine, Saturday morning in

June; Amber's next order of business was to locate her eight-year-old-daughter, Trista. Surely Trista was outside on this fine, Saturday morning in June. Before running downstairs, Amber peeked her head into Paulette's bedroom, "I'm going to the store. You'll be alright for about an hour?"

With greasy hair, scummy teeth and still in her sleepwear; Paulette nodded.

"I'll give you a bath when I get home. Just sit tight. I have some things to do this morning."

And Amber had things to do yesterday, and the day before that. Paulette was now going on three days without a bath or having her teeth brushed. She remained in the same nightgown for nearly three days and was beginning notice her own stink. Even worse, Paulette hadn't been downstairs in three days—the last time being Wednesday when Father left for his golf outing. In recent times, Paulette wished her father had more time to be at home. It would appear that Father's absence brought with it some neglect on Amber's part. But she couldn't blame Amber for not going downstairs this time. Somehow the chairlift broke while bringing Paulette up the stairs on Wednesday night. Fortunately the lift made it to the top of the stairs!

Most of Amber's neglect and hidden resentment wasn't done on purpose. With Trista getting older, there were new obligations as there are for any parent. As a toddler, it was easy to care for Trista along with Paulette. Although certainly challenging at times—up late at night with a sick child, dealing with temper tantrums, etc—a toddler's needs are simpler than a kid in grammar school. A toddler only needs Mother to be near, showing affection, providing food or changing a diaper. But Trista now had new demands for her mother. Not only did she require help with homework and needed to discuss conflicts or silly happenings at school; there was an increasing demand for Amber to come to the school assemblies and support Trista in her sudden interest in extracurricular activities. Caring for an invalid, twenty-three-year-old, adopted daughter took a backseat. Aside from that, Amber wouldn't have Trista feeling that she was second best.

Just as expected, Trista was outside enjoying her jumbo playground. Her favorite activity in recent times: practicing penny drops from the monkey bars. Tumbling was every Tuesday and Thursday night, and Trista was very proud at her ability to do an advanced exercise.

"Come-on, Trista, let's go to the store."

"Awe, how long are we going to be gone?"

"Not long, about an hour."

* * *

Just as expected, the Saturday grocery store was a regular meat market of gorgeous women who browsed the aisles in their finest, sexy attire—some of them screaming for attention just as Amber did. To eliminate the competition, Amber tried going to the store on Friday nights, but men usually didn't shop on Fridays.

While picking out fruit for the week, Amber felt and soon noticed the chubby, shaggy-shoe-horse-bald produce manager with cheesy moustache watching her. That wasn't exactly what she had in mind. He'd give any woman attention; even force it on her like some creepy stalker. Was there anyone younger and more appealing?

Although quick to give a barely-noticeable glance, younger men were usually in the honeymoon phase of their marriage and walked very close to their wives. In fact, a younger man seemed to follow his wife around like a lost puppy dog. A newlywed wife appeared to have had quite enough of her new husband and it was time to enforce who was boss in the marriage. Only showing kindness in rare moments, a newlywed wife was… well, a spoiled, little bitch. These young women had no idea how nice they had it. Amber would have gladly traded her absent, gray-haired, old-man husband for a younger, loving man who only wished to enjoy his wife.

Further walking along the aisles was like a gallery that illustrated the progressive stages of marriage that might have caused Amber to consider where she stood in the order of chaos. People were so wonderfully in love before getting married. But then a newlywed wife, who left the comfort of mom and dad's wing, might have become unreasonably disappointed with her new life and projected haughtiness towards her husband. A couple kids later might have transformed her into a worn, haggard and miserably plump woman who dressed in sloppy sweatpants and a dirty, messy shirt. And this was the sort of wife who was accompanied by the good-looking hunk in his early thirties. A small child sat in the shopping cart and another clung to his wife's shirttail while walking beside her. Although her husband was attentive and did what he could to make the morning easier, he could sense a considerable animosity from his wife. What ever happened to the tenderness and romance of earlier years? Why couldn't he reach her? Why did she fight him so?

She was too worn out to enjoy her marriage. And this obviously showed as her husband soon took notice of Amber. That was the sort of man who Amber wished attention from! His chemistry announced how he wanted her so badly as his deep, bedroom eyes locked with Amber's. But Amber was safe. He was with his wife, and wouldn't dare approach the exciting woman. Amber merely smiled and walked past while giving her ass a little twitch—some eye-candy to be seen and not touched.

And all these things took place on a Saturday morning in June: haughty, newlywed wives; bitter, resentful and haggard moms; and women like Amber who pranced about the store while silently begging for attention. Perhaps women were better off in the old days when a fat, beer-chugging slob would dictate,

"You're not going anywhere! Stay home!" Did women feel more loved and appreciated, then?

* * *

Rest assured, Paulette received her long, overdue bath just before lunch and had her teeth lightly grazed with the toothbrush.

"Your Father is coming home, tomorrow." said Amber.

Thank God for that! At least Paulette would have a brief moment of daily hygiene while Father was in between business trips, conventions or golf outings. Paulette considered advising Father of the mistreatment that started in recent years. But she feared punishment from Amber when Father went away. Even still, what if Amber left? Would there come a day when Paulette would be dumped in a nursing home because Father was busy? Unfortunately, this question only spawned further concerns for Paulette of her future. There would certainly be a day when Father would be gone and possibly Amber. How could Paulette prepare for her future?

Chapter Twenty

By Sunday morning, the wheelchair lift magically worked again! "Maybe something was shorted." was Amber's quick and easy answer. Whatever the reason, it was now possible for Paulette to come downstairs, cleaned and dressed in fresh clothes to wait for Father's return.

There was no point in wishing as it wouldn't come true. Although Amber would have wanted her husband to return home in the morning—hours before dinner—Michael was scheduled to return home in the late afternoon. Surely this would mean a quick greeting and brief peck to Amber's lips before visiting a moment with Paulette and Trista. Then he would ask of what's for dinner. Upon hearing the answer he would announce going down into the cellar for a bottle of wine. Amber once tried pulling a bottle of wine from the cellar before Michael came home. But sure enough, it wasn't the type or flavor that he wished for that night. It was necessary for Michael to hand pick his own bottle upon returning home from a trip, which usually took about an hour-and-half.

Just as predicted, the musical horn from the limousine tooted on that Sunday afternoon as Michael returned.

He entered the door, "Hi, Honey! I missed you." He gave Amber a brief peck to the lips and then entered the family room where Paulette sat. "How's my girl?"

Paulette smiled in return as she received a kiss on the cheek. Amber called up the stairs, "Trista, Dad's home!"

Trista galloped down the stairs, "Daddy!" Upon hugging her stepfather, she excitedly informed him of how well she could do penny drops.

"Really? Well that's great! I'm proud of you!" Then Michael asked Amber the usual question. "What's for dinner?"

"I've got chicken marinating in the refrigerator. I was waiting for you to come home before putting it on the grill."

"That sounds great! I'll go down into the wine cellar and pull a bottle for dinner."

But this only meant that Amber should wait about an hour before putting the chicken on the grill. Gone for nearly five days, Michael apparently felt it was best to pay a visit to Linsey's chamber some four-hundred feet below the wine cellar. Most likely he would return with a half-empty bottle of some Pinot Noir and a full wine glass that would be dumped into the sink.

This was just another one of those things that added to Amber's unhappiness as a wife. She wondered how long it would take for a husband in mourning to get over the loss of his wife. She presumed maybe a year-or-two before all would be well. But going on eight years, their anniversary in just two weeks, Amber still felt the presence of Linsey in her home.

Consider the hypothetical example of a woman only a few months from presenting her husband with divorce papers, but is surprised with his unexpected death. How devastated she is. How she sobs at his funeral and lays a rose on his coffin while crying out, "I love you!" She might even confess some months later to sleeping on his side of the bed and often praying and seeking his guidance. It's sad, really, how death restores the years to those early moments of falling in love. If your wife hates you and constantly nags, don't worry. She will love you with all her heart as you lay in the casket.

If death can restore love to a bitter marriage, imagine the effect it has on a man or woman who loved a spouse so dearly. The fact is a deceased husband or wife will continue to be loved. You can never compete with a dead person! Expect photos, souvenirs and sentimental gifts to continue to be displayed in the home for years to come. Instead of competing with the deceased spouse, why not treat your lover with care and befriend the beloved departed while showing respect? He or she is in a better place and wishes only the best for you. At troubled times you can even ask the departed, "Did he or she do this with you as well? How did you deal with it?" You'd be surprised how an answer is most often given.

Unfortunately, Amber did not understand this. And this might have been half of her problem all those years. But then it certainly was odd of Michael to have made a death mask of Linsey and then develop it into a statue-head to be adored as some relic that appeared to grant the power of clairvoyance. Pictures and a few souvenirs is one thing. But to treat a piece of morbid artwork as if it were somehow an incarnation of a deceased spouse, then place it in a chamber to be visited in near worship would be enough to disturb anyone.

Ten minutes after six o'clock, Amber stood outside, flipping the chicken on the grill. Upon returning from the basement, Michael brought with him a half-empty bottle of Pinot Noir and a full wine glass that was carefully dumped into the sink.

Michael's eyes darted at Amber, "So what was wrong with wheelchair lift?"

This surprised Amber. She didn't recall making mention of it. "Huh? Oh yeah, it stopped working Wednesday night and then started up again this morning."

"So it stopped on the night I left town, and then started working on the day of my return?"

Amber maintained a blank stare.

"Hmmm…" Michael quickly walked over to the stairs and operated the lift while following it up to the second level and back down again. "Well it seems fine. I don't notice it being off track or any burning smells."

Amber further added, "I know, it's weird. Maybe there was a short or something. Maybe we should have someone come out and take a look."

Michael said nothing else and walked over to the patio door. "Is the chicken almost done?"

"I just flipped them over before you came up."

Michael then ordered, "Well why don't you go outside and see if they're almost ready. It smells like they're burning."

This was another small item that contributed to Amber's sudden dislike of her husband of seven years. Once-upon-a-time he would excitedly asked, "Mmmmm… What's for dinner?" To whatever answer given, he would surely exclaim, "It smells delicious. I can't wait!" But now he only asked the question in such a way to make sure Amber did her wifely duties. It wasn't uncommon for Michael to complain of how it was being cooked, or demand that she check to see if it was done.

While outside, Amber soon realized why she was ordered out of the house. She concluded that Michael was asking Paulette about the recent days of his absence. In fact, Paulette probably made mention of the wheelchair lift while Michael initially greeted her. The two often spoke through facial expressions and near intuition. That was the only explanation Amber had for Michael's sudden knowledge of the wheelchair lift.

* * *

For over seven years, Amber hadn't a morning when she could just sleep in. Caring for both Trista and Paulette required that she rise early. Even with Trista on summer break, and enjoying her new schedule of sleeping in late, it was still necessary for Amber to awake early and care for Paulette.

Strange things were beginning to happen in the Dickly castle. There was almost a subtle energy of change that was soon to lead to disaster. If you've ever examined the days in retrospect to a sudden crisis or catastrophe, you might have noticed many mishaps along the way—indicators that could point to something about to happen.

On that Monday morning after Michael's return, a small indicator light flagged trouble in the Dickly castle. In the middle of preparing Paulette for her bath, Amber soon galloped down the stairs and into the kitchen where Michael poured his first cup of morning coffee. "Michael?"

"What?"

"There's no hot water."

"No hot water? What do you mean?"

"I was filling up Paulette's bath water and it's cold. There's no hot water."

In the middle of taking a sip of coffee, Michael nearly slammed the cup down on the counter. "Oh for cripes sake, Amber! What are you talking about, now? What the hell is going on around here? First the wheelchair lift won't work, and now we have no hot water?" Michael slapped the kitchen faucet to the hot water position and wacked the water on as if smacking someone in the face. His finger trembled in outrage while under the water, gauging the truth in what Amber was reporting.

Amber watched in disbelief at her husband's behavior. It was in that moment that Amber realized she was married to a grumpy, old man. He was certainly not the person she fell in love with.

Then he pounded the faucet back down with a hammer fist while speaking words of vile blasphemy, asking God to curse those things which were already in a poor state. Michael growled at his young and beautiful wife, "Can't you take care of the house like a wife is supposed to do? I mean can't you take care of this? There's no hot water! So call a freaking plumber! I've got a business to run and don't have time to waste at the dingbat farm!" Michael stormed back upstairs.

And so the young and beautiful Amber was nothing more than a dingbat who couldn't function as a housewife. The last time Amber heard the word dingbat would have been some late night rerun of All in the Family. Did her husband really see a comparison between Amber and Edith Bunker?

Although in further resentment of her husband and very close to deciding she no longer loved him, Amber looked through the phonebook for what appeared to be a decent plumber. She always felt that the first ad in the section of a phonebook was an indicator of a professional business. But the first plumbing company advertised was a good hour away. It was necessary to follow the page down until finding one located in Mapleview. Mapleview wasn't far from Sillmac, so that was the plumber who received the call on a Monday morning in June. Amber was promised to have a visit by about eleven o'clock that morning.

In the meantime, poor Paulette was informed of the inconvenience. "…unless you want to take a cold bath."

Paulette shook her head, no.

Of course Amber wasn't going to start the morning unwashed. With a visitor coming, she had to be in her best appearance. Amber washed her long, beautiful hair while being careful not to make contact with the cold water as best as possible. Then she sponged herself down in the shower and quickly rinsed while shivering. How lucky I am to be the narrator. For only I can see Amber's beautiful, naked skin with goose bumps and many other treasures left to imagination.

While Amber dried off, Michael rudely entered and announced his need to do morning sit-down business. And of course he had to crudely ask, "What are you taking a shower for? Can't you wait a couple hours? Do you have somewhere important to go today?"

Amber remained silent while thinking to herself, "It's better than being a miserable, stinky, old man!"

Amber dressed in the bedroom while Michael did his business behind the closed bathroom door. While Amber brushed her hair in the bedroom mirror, Michael emerged upon the sound of the toilet flushing—hadn't even washed his hands! The bathroom always stinks when a man does sit-down business. This is why most of us kindly spray aerosol, turn on the fan and shut the door while exiting. But Michael left the door wide open so that the vilest stench that one might expect to smell in the nursing home wafted into the bedroom, nearly causing Amber to gag.

Amber exclaimed, "Pew!"

The old man was proud of what he birthed. "What, you think you smell like a rose?"

Again, Amber remained silent while thinking to herself, "At least I wash my hands and spray aerosol when I'm done."

Lately, Michael had a problem with Amber's appearance. He watched as his young and beautiful wife applied lip gloss then asked, "Why do you have to dress up every day? Every time I see you, you're in some cute, tight-ass jeans or shorts and a nice top. I mean it would be nice to have a normal wife that dresses in normal clothes."

Amber was finally at rope's end as she put the lip gloss down. "A normal wife; like a grumpy, old, fat, miserable hag? She'd be the perfect match for you!" Then Amber stormed out of the bedroom and back downstairs.

* * *

Just as promised, the doorbell rang at five minutes to eleven o'clock. With Michael upstairs in his office, Amber rushed over to the door to answer. Her heart nearly stopped and her face flushed when she saw who the plumber was. The gorgeous hunk who accompanied his miserable, haggard wife in the grocery store on Saturday now stood at Amber's doorstep. If you recall, Amber took great delight in exchanging deep, bedroom eyes with him on Saturday and twitching her ass while walking away. She was safe in that moment as his wife was nearby. But Amber was in trouble, now. Not only was the gorgeous hunk away from his wife, but he remembered Amber, as evidenced by the mischievous smile in his eyes.

"Hi, you called for a plumber?" Now he was asking to come in!

"Uh, yeah, we're having trouble with our hot water." Amber stepped aside and motioned the plumber to enter while her eyes remained fixed to the floor.

"I'm Alex." He extended his muscular arm.

Amber finally looked up and took his hand for a brief, business shake.

"And you are?" It was so rude of the sexy, delicious, little lady not to introduce herself.

"Amber; Amber Dickly."

"Dickly? As in Dickly's Hardware?"

Amber smiled and nodded.

"No offense, but your stuff is way, too overpriced!"

"Uh, that's my husband's business. I've never even stepped in a Dickly's." Perhaps mention of her husband would have restored Amber's safety.

But Alex didn't care about Mr. Dickly. He asked with a playful grin, "If your husband owns a chain of hardware stores, why can't he fix the hot water?"

It was a good question in Amber's mind. "Well, he's upstairs in his office doing busy things."

"Oh, I get it; the business guy that doesn't know how to use tools?" Making a couple potshots at Amber's husband certainly strengthened his ego and confidence, enough for Alex to get down to business. "So why don't we look at the most logical thing, first. Have you checked your hot water heater?"

Amber shrugged her shoulders and shook her head, no.

"Okay, can you show me where your hot water heater is?"

"Ummm… it's probably in the basement."

Clearly, the sexy, delicious, little lady was clueless of anything mechanical. She was just Alex's type! He asked, "Can you bring me to your basement?"

"Sure!" Amber motioned the plumber to follow, this time being extra careful not to twitch her ass under the cute, denim shorts.

It was almost as if Alex could instinctively locate the utility room in the basement. Although Amber hadn't the first clue of where it could be located, Alex nearly led her to the room once downstairs. He opened the door, flipped on the light and then examined the hot water heater for a moment. "Well what do you know about that?"

Amber was suddenly nervous. "What? Did you find something?"

"*Yeah*! The valve that allows water to the hot water heater is closed. There's no water coming in. Are you sure no one was down here before?"

"Not that I know of."

Alex wore a queer expression and then turned the valve open. "We should wait a few minutes to check for hot water. Are you sure maybe your husband wasn't down here?"

It just wouldn't have been a logical explanation. Considering Michael's behavior, he was very surprised—extremely irate—that there was suddenly no hot water. And Amber certainly didn't close the valve. She wouldn't have known the first thing about it. "No one was down here as far as I know."

Waiting some minutes before checking for hot water would have left plenty of time for an activity that Alex so badly wanted. But he wasn't sure about the customer. She seemed so uneasy with his presence. With such uncertainty, Alex would have to follow plan B. He spent a few minutes with Amber in the utility room, explaining the anatomy of the hot water heater, sometimes drawing close with no other purpose but to feel her energy and smell her scent.

Plan B was unfavorable for Alex. In reality, he never executed plan A or plan B, but rehearsed them in recent time in case ever needing them. Plan B was less aggressive, more subtle and left the ball in a customer's court. After finally verifying that hot water had been restored to the Dickly Castle, Alex pulled out his business card with direct, emergency number. "Here's my card. If anything ever comes up—*anything*, leaky pipes or *maybe the valve for your hot water heater is suddenly closed*—you give me a call. Call me anytime, day or night. I'll be sure to answer." Then his eyes smiled so mischievously, hoping the customer would get the message.

The ball was now in Amber's court.

Chapter Twenty-one

A couple weeks passed since the incident with the hot water heater. Michael and Amber celebrated their eight-year anniversary together that was nothing spectacular, just a nice dinner out and some more jewelry from Michael as a gift. But it did surpass seven years together, which surely meant both husband and wife made it through the seven-year itch.

But Amber certainly itched while laying in her bed, alone, on a night when Michael was away on business. Sex wasn't all that great in recent months—actually in the past couple years. Michael was becoming increasingly unappealing. Due to her husband's old age, it was beginning to feel for Amber that sex was being had with her father. Michael's breath was beginning to remind her of some crotchety, old man. And although she did her best to overlook these small items for the sake of intimacy with her husband, Michael was having increasing difficulty with performance. The man was overworked and neglected to care for himself. He ate much, too well while on the road. His stomach grew into more than just a cute pouch that a lovable hubby might develop in older years. Rather, it was like having a partially-deflated beach ball wedged in between her and Michael. High cholesterol and blood pressure was causing circulation problems for the old man. Although beta blockers and cholesterol medicine significantly corrected a potentially dangerous health problem, Michael's testosterone levels were in serious decline as he obviously reached andropause (menopause for men). To put it bluntly, the man needed help "getting it up" in bed. Thankfully, Michael's doctor determined that he was healthy enough for sexual activity. But although male performance drugs were safe to use, intimacy required extended foreplay—servicing Michael for bothersome periods of time, if you will—which usually led to frustration and irritability for Michael as he complained that Amber wasn't doing it right. She often wondered if Michael was really into sex anymore.

Sex was just no fun, at all, for Amber! Ashamed, she sometimes recalled younger years when some boy would make out with her and rub his swollen desperation against her thigh. And before Trista was born, Amber enjoyed exhilarating sex with Matt (Trista's father). In younger years, guys were always ready for Amber. And although she hadn't thought much of it then, looking back, it felt so good to be wanted and desired.

Who else might have appeared in Amber's imagination while stirring restlessly in bed? Desiring a young man so strongly, Amber suddenly imagined the plumber. Alex was so muscular, so much more appealing than her crotchety, old husband. It would only be necessary to touch Amber, and the flames would ignite between them. Alex left his business card with emergency number, even emphasized answering a silly call brought on by a sudden closing of the valve to the hot water heater. The ball was in Amber's court. But why was she so hesitant?

For another fifteen minutes she lay in bed, restlessly stirring, breathing heavily and wishing so badly to be man-handled by Alex. It was 12:20 am and much, too late for a call to a plumber. But then Alex did emphasize answering her call day or night. Shivering from nervousness, she finally arose from bed and pulled Alex's business card that was buried at the bottom of her lingerie drawer. Amber quietly descended the stairs to the main level. She was so crazy for following through with the plan. This is what she continued to remind herself while further descending into the basement, where she entered the utility closet and closed the incoming valve to the hot water heater. Finally, Amber reached for the phone and called her plumber, mentioning a sudden loss of hot water.

Wearing nothing but one of Linsey's summer nightgowns, Amber stood outside at the entryway of the Dickly castle, and waited for the arrival of Alex the plumber. As he pulled into the oversized, horseshoe driveway, Amber imagined his headlights shining light through the material of her nightgown and revealing secret treasures that beckoned for his play.

"Good evening! You lost hot water, again?"

Suddenly, Amber was pulled out of her desperate fantasy and realized that she summoned a man into her home and showed obvious intention to be seduced. She was in trouble, now! "Yes, I'm sorry. It stopped working, again."

"Well didn't you show your husband the incoming valve?"

"He's not home…" Uh-oh! Why did Amber reveal this to the plumber? She was going to have to keep her mouth shut as much as possible and quickly escort him out of the house once the problem had been resolved.

Once inside the house, Amber took notice of his more-than four o'clock shadow. Obviously, Alex hadn't shaven since yesterday morning which further added to his sex appeal. But Amber was too frightened, nearly trembling at her realization of stupidity. What was wrong with Amber? She should have completed her lonely moment under the covers and then forgot about the plumber like any good wife does.

The most obvious thing was to be checked, first. Alex whispered, realizing others may have been sleeping, "Well, let's take a look at your hot water heater."

In nothing but Linsey's summer nightgown, Amber escorted Alex down the stairs. Does a woman have any idea how irresistible she looks in a nearly-transparent nightgown? Going on three weeks without sex from his own wife, Alex just about exploded in his pants at the sight of Amber's shapely buttocks that rocked, twisted and jiggled while walking ahead.

Amber could feel the predatory instincts from behind. She needed to get Alex out of the house as quickly as possible! "Oh, stupid me! I just remembered! I bet that valve is closed. I should have checked it before I gave you a call."

"I bet it is." Alex coldly replied.

Amber reached in the utility closet and opened the valve. "There, I fixed it. I'm sorry for bothering you." The silhouette of her naked breasts and nipples pushed through Linsey's nightgown. Amber's flushed face with crazed eyes and nearly-swollen lips said everything in opposite for Alex to leave.

"Let me just make sure you turned it in the right direction. Sometimes people get confused." Alex approached the utility room which brought him closer to Amber. "Here, let me show you something." He took hold of Amber's delicate wrist and pulled it towards the incoming valve of the hot water heater. "Always remember, you turn left to open it and right to close it." He placed her hand on the valve while keeping his own on top. Then he slowly guided Amber's trembling grip on the valve. "There's an old saying I remember. Lefty-loosey… righty-tighty… lefty-loosey… righty-tighty."

If Alex's motion and voice wasn't hinting towards sensual, then his other hand that rested on Amber's tail bone, soon to be her buttocks, gave clear indication of what was to happen next.

All female species in the animal kingdom play a similar game. They hide in secluded areas in heat, dripping with an overpowering desire to be taken by a male. She comes out of hiding for a brief moment and shakes her tail in a male suitor's face. But then instinctively she becomes frightened and runs away to hide. "I wasn't coming on to you! I wasn't trying to communicate anything to you! You imagined those signals." She'll deny everything, of course.

But sometimes an unfortunate female will find herself alone and cornered with her male suitor. In this moment, the game is over. Trembling and nearly hyperventilating, her resistance only adds to the rapture.

It had been some years since Amber experienced a young man her own age. Alex's body was so hard and strong; and, unlike Michael, Alex was ready from the moment the nightgown was aggressively pulled off. With her body pushed against the hot water heater, Amber's resisting arms were merely a way of gauging and admiring the plumber's strength. Alex was so damn strong and there was no fighting off what he wanted. Amber's fragile hands were simply held against the pipes while his shadowy whiskers coarsely grazed across her delicate neck as the plumber devoured the scrumptious, little lady with hot kisses. The kisses were the only thing needed for Amber to finally surrender.

Soon escorted to the center of the basement, Amber found herself next lying propped up against the basement bar. In those moments, she couldn't help but realize that this is what she needed for so long. How glad Amber was, finally, to have given her plumber a late night call.

Although tonight was everything she ever wished for, Amber couldn't help but realize that she would need much more. Many wives have a secret friend to care for those needs that a husband can't fulfill. Perhaps it was best to elevate the new relationship with Alex to a friendship and get to know him. "My husband is out of town for the week. Actually, he's on the road a lot. Why don't you come over tomorrow night for a late dinner and some drinks? Get to know each other, you know?"

Alex paused for a moment. Feeling guilty of his first, ever, intimate moment with a customer—not to mention his first moment of infidelity—it was difficult to receive Amber's suggestion as a good idea. But then reasoning soon took over. Sex was had maybe once every six weeks between Alex and his wife. Not only that, closeness and communication was becoming increasingly difficult in his marriage; due to Alex's, wife's bitterness. Why shouldn't he have accepted a new friend who just so happened to enjoy occasional sex? Amber's suggestion was probably the best thing Alex heard in weeks.

"Sure, you want me to wait until your kids go down for the night. Just give me another late night, emergency call. You're right; we should get to know each other."

* * *

The Dickly castle was a huge home and a place one could easily entertain a guest. But there was a small problem when it came to Amber entertaining a secret lover late at night. Neither Trista nor Paulette should have been aware of the strange man in the home—*definitely* not Paulette, for obvious reasons. But the solution was simple as the Dickly castle had a large basement that was an impressive living area, fully carpeted and finished with elaborate furnishings and full bar. On Alex and Amber's "first real date", they sat downstairs at the bar, enjoying carryout Chinese and mixed drinks. And although only their first date, Amber and Alex were already the best-of-friends.

Loosened up from a couple drinks, Amber began to speak of her domestic problems. "I don't have anything against her. I mean I love Paulette like my own daughter, but it's time consuming to have to take care of her. Trista needs attention, too, and sometimes I just need a break from caring for an invalid. Some days I just want to leave her up there.—you know? She can go a day without a bath."

Alex agreed, "Absolutely! She should be able to understand that."

Amber continued, "The last time my husband went away, I told Paulette that the wheelchair lift wasn't working—just a little white lie. Maybe it was too obvious that it suddenly started working on the day my husband came home. But that little bitch had to tell her father. He got all bent out of shape and in my face that the wheelchair lift was fine." Amber sighed. "Sometimes I just want to get away.—you know? I've been pretty much confined to this house ever since I met my husband. We go away on trips as a family, but when was the last time Michael and I just went away, the two of us? Never!"

Towards the end of Amber's rant, Alex gently took her hand and stroked his thumb against it. Then he concluded the conversation with, "Yeah, sometimes you just need a little break from it all. I feel the same way. I guess that's why people like you and me make friends. And thanks to your huge bar down here, we can definitely get away—if you know what I mean." Alex winked while reaching for both their glasses and then poured another round of drinks for him and Amber.

"Isn't your wife going to notice you coming home, smelling like booze?"

"Nah! She won't care! Even if she does say something, I'll just tell her that the customer was some old man who mixed up a few drinks once the job was done."

About another half hour of drinking, lively talking and laughter went by. Amber hadn't loosened up like this since before she met Michael. Alex was truly a wonderful person to have in her life, even if she had just met the man. Amber's face was numb and the words just poured out, nearly stuttering and slurring. But as far as Amber could determine, she was hiding her drunkenness quite well. And then she began to speak more of Paulette. "I just wish I knew of some way to sabotage that darn wheelchair lift. I've had so much to drink; I might not want to deal with her in the morning."

Alex took a final gulp of his mixed drink and then reached over to the refrigerator for a beer-chaser. "You want to know how to break that wheelchair lift so that it's convincing to your husband?"

Amber sat motionless for a split second with a beaming smile on her face. In her stillness, one could notice that she was heavily buzzed as evidenced by the slight dizzying motion of her neck. Amber giggled, "Get out of here! Are you serious? You know how to break that thing?"

Alex took a hearty swig from his bottle of beer and then set it on the bar. Halfcocked and loaded with confidence, he was a real boy scout that earned more than his share of merits in life. You know the type. "I can get that thing to malfunction *and* make it look like we didn't do it. But what's in it for me?" He knew the night would end in his favor, regardless. But Alex wished to up the ante, make it feel as though he rightfully earned the night's end.

Amber slowly circumnavigated the glass with her finger and smiled seductively. "We'll just have to see about that."

Rest assured, Alex and Amber were as quiet as mice when upstairs—at least they thought this. Perhaps they should have finished the party for the night in the basement while allowing the booze to wear off. With a good handle on their drunkenness, the two nearly staggered across the foyer, and Amber fell into Alex's toolbox which made a loud rattle. The drunken mishap was followed by giggles. The noise was loud enough to awaken Paulette, who now lay in bed, attempting to gauge the activities downstairs.

She listened carefully while piecing together the scene. A man's voice who was not Father's was eager to play with the wheelchair lift. "Wait! I want to ride it down the stairs. I've always wanted to try this." Amber could be heard giggling while the wheelchair lift motor softly hummed. Obviously the strange man was riding it down the stairs, then back up again.

"Can this thing go faster?"

Amber giggled, "Faster?"

"Yeah, you can make it go fast and eject her out the window."

Amber giggled all the louder as if her sides were about to split.

Alex quickly shushed her, reminding Amber that Paulette was in the next room. Then he whispered, "We should really bring this thing to the bottom of the stairs so we don't wake anyone up."

Once at the bottom level, Alex carefully examined the wheelchair lift, in particular, the area that appeared to receive main power. It was covered by a large, metal plate that was secured by a dozen screws.

Alex had just the tool in his large box. Like any real man, Alex had only the best: a high-powered, Makita, cordless drill with Philips bit to remove the screws. Alex was definitely the man Amber needed to know. And he was definitely the man qualified to tamper with a wheelchair lift, as everyone knows that a plumber is an expert on matters pertaining to electricity. Not only that, Alex could disable the wheelchair lift *and* make it look as though no one tampered with it.

He placed the bit at the first screw head. But the drunken fool that he was, Alex held the drill at an angle and firmly pressed the trigger. It only resulted in a rattling, stripping noise that widened the head of the screw. The head was now close to impossible to accommodate any kind of bit or screwdriver.

"Son of a... I stripped the screw head." But Alex could get around this problem. He reached in the tool box for a wide flat blade that barely locked in place of the screw head. With a little elbow grease, he pushed in while turning counterclockwise. "Lefty-loosey... righty-tighty..." All Amber could notice was his mighty biceps flexing as he carefully turned the screw.

Now you think that Alex would have been more careful with the remaining screws. Perhaps he would have put the Makita, cordless drill away and used an old fashioned screwdriver to prevent any further stripping of screws. But he was a man; and no man would bother removing eleven screws by hand. Alex could operate a cordless drill. He could do this!

But just as before, his drunken state caused the drill to be positioned at an angle so that another screw head had been stripped. "Son of a… I did it again!"

In the meantime, Paulette listened carefully from her bed, upstairs. She knew what was happening. Some strange man was tampering with the wheelchair lift.

"I'm going to have to use a regular screwdriver for the rest of 'em."

Amber watched, nearly drooling, as Alex's mighty biceps continuously rotated the handle of the screwdriver counterclockwise. At some point, she placed her hand on his flexed muscle. She just had to feel it working!

Finally, the last screw had been removed which enabled the plate cover to be taken off. The plumber carefully examined the internal circuitry and determined that shorting the incoming 120 volts would most likely cause significant damage to the circuit board.

Alex warned Amber, "This is where it's going to get dangerous. You might want to step back." He had just the right tool for this dangerous part of the job. Alex reached for a pair of needle nose pliers that had rubber-gripped handles, and then put on a work glove for extra protection. In all his cleverness, he used the needle nose pliers to short the incoming power at the circuit board. Surely this would cause damage!

And everyone knows how predictable electricity can be! Perhaps Alex calculated that the damage would occur only at the circuit board. But shorting the incoming power caused heavy sparks and an arc that discharged out towards the light, oak, wooden railing and created a burn to the wood!

You really have to hand it to Alex! Stripping the heads of two screws and causing damage; not only to the enclosed circuit board, but the wooden railing as well; certainly made it appear as though the wheelchair lift hadn't been tampered with! And anyone sober enough would further consider that the wheelchair lift had been damaged at the bottom of the stairs while Paulette was in her room. Why would it be downstairs when Paulette was left upstairs?

It was still a job well done for Amber. The plumber closed the metal plate and cleaned up after his work. Then the two went back into the basement where Alex received payment for his night's work.

Chapter Twenty-two

Badly hung over with a throbbing headache, Amber awoke around 10:45 the following morning. This was a good four hours past the usual time when she awoke to care for Paulette. Surely, Paulette would be a bitch this morning. And speaking of Paulette, did the plumber actually blow up the wheelchair lift last night?

Amber jumped out of bed and walked diagonally while adjusting to the dizziness. She had to get downstairs and examine the damage to the wheelchair lift. But then there was Paulette to consider. Being that Paulette was closer, Amber entered her room first.

"Hey…"

Paulette lay in bed with a bitter look.

"I know; I slept in late this morning. Sorry! You don't have to look at me that way!" Amber wheeled the crane device over. "Let's get you in the bathroom so you can do your business." But when pulling back Paulette's covers, Amber discovered that the blankets, bed sheet, a portion of the mattress as well as the lower portion of Paulette's sleepwear were soaking wet. Paulette had urinated in bed, probably in agony and frustration of having to wait longer than usual to use the toilet.

"You peed in your bed? Come on Paulette, I don't feel like dealing with this crap this morning! Why would you do that?"

The look on Paulette's face said, "Sorry, what did you expect me to do?"

"Damn it, anyway!" Amber ripped the blanket and sheet off the bed and threw it on the floor. The smell of fresh urine enveloped the air. "I should really just make you lay there all day in your own pee!" Amber almost mentioned her desire to send Paulette into a nursing home. Instead, she yanked the sheet out from under Paulette and threw it in the collection of urine-soaked bedding. Then she carefully pulled off Paulette's nightwear and added it to the heap on the floor.

"I'm not touching this! Let me go down into the laundry room and get a basket." No longer dizzy, but in a terrible mood, Amber climbed down the stairs and then stopped in dread at the sight of the wheelchair lift. There along the light, oak railing were several burn marks near the electrical plate. To make matters worse, two screw heads on the plate were noticeably stripped. It was certainly apparent that someone tampered with the wheelchair lift.

"Oh my gosh! What did he do?" How in the world was Amber going to explain this to her husband?

Just then, Trista entered the foyer, munching on a Pop Tart. "Mommy? What were you and that man doing last night?"

Adrenaline spiked through Amber's veins. "What man?"

"The man that was with you. I saw him riding up and down the stairs on Paulette's lift."

"Trista, you were dreaming! There was no one here! And I don't ever want to hear you say that again, you understand?"

Trista nodded while continuing to munch on her Pop Tart. Then she boldly asked, "What happened? Why is the railing burned?"

"I don't know, Honey. It looks like Paulette's lift is broken."

"Did that man do it, Mommy?"

Amber had all she could take of her daughter's keen observations. She took hold of Trista's face, "I'm not going to tell you again; there was no man here last night."

* * *

Paulette made herself appear disappointed that the wheelchair lift was broken. But she was really masking her anger, realizing that Amber was having an affair on Father. She didn't appreciate the joke of being ejected out the window, and she certainly didn't appreciate the fact that a strange man was invited in the home to damage her lift. But how could she tell Father? He was so busy with work and depended on Amber to care for her. If Amber left, what would become of Paulette?

As the days in Michael's absence passed, Amber's mood swung from anxiety to forced relaxation. She went through every possible scenario of what to tell Michael. She even considered having the railing repaired before Michael came home. But any attempt to cover the damage would look just like that—an attempt to cover damage. It was best to leave the wheelchair lift as-is and appear clueless as to how it would have ended up in that condition. But even then, there was a big problem. Why was the lift downstairs while Paulette was upstairs? The usual custom was to leave the lift at the top of the stairs at night, and leave it downstairs while Paulette was on the lower level. Could the tracking of the lift have suddenly lost grip and slid down the railing where it exploded? Could Amber lead Michael into believing this?

By Saturday midmorning, the limousine tooted its musical horn, announcing Michael's return. As usual, Michael gave his wife a brief peck to the lips and then turned towards the family room to greet Paulette.

"Where's Paulette?"

"She's upstairs. We had another problem with the wheelchair lift."

"What? What happened, now?" Michael stormed over to the staircase and then growled, "For cripes sake! What the hell happened? Look at the railing! How did it get burned?"

Amber did her best to mask nervousness. "I don't know. I came down one morning and found it like this. It looks like it exploded or something."

"Exploded? How?" Michael bent down to closely examine the area of the burn. Then he investigated the wheelchair lift and immediately took notice of the stripped screw heads. "Did you call someone out here to look at the lift?"

Amber answered, "No."

"Did you try opening something up?"

"No."

Michael shook his head and sighed. "I mean what the hell goes on around here while I'm gone? I come home and see a broken lift and burns all over the railing." He ascended the stairway, obviously on his way to see Paulette. Amber trailed behind.

As Michael entered Paulette's room, Amber stood in the hallway, but watched carefully the activities between father and daughter.

"Hi, Honey. Is your wheelchair lift broken?"

Paulette sadly nodded, yes.

Michael kissed his daughter on the cheek. "Don't worry; Daddy will get someone out here to fix it. I wish I could carry you downstairs, but I'm getting old." Michael wouldn't dare mention the other reason. In the years of Paulette's inactivity, she gained a considerable amount of weight so that anyone would have difficulty carrying her down a flight of stairs. But Paulette didn't need to know this. Instead, Father was a gentleman and kindly took all the blame for Paulette's confinement.

The rest of the morning and throughout the afternoon was mostly quiet. Michael's silence was an indicator of sorting through his thoughts and feelings. Most likely, he was angry with Amber; but hadn't decided on how to act on his suspicions.

Occasionally, Amber's cell phone would buzz in her pocket; to which she would quickly remove it and begin typing away at the keypad. This was a very, unusual behavior; and for some reason, it disturbed Michael. In fact, the more he observed Amber in her tight-ass jeans and cutesy blouse; slowly pacing the rooms, creeping around walls and typing away at her phone; the more silently outraged Michael became. Was there some new technology on the phone that enabled Amber to have a secret boyfriend? Remember, this was only 2003. Texting wasn't as widespread as it is today.

Then, near four o'clock in the afternoon, Michael spoke up. "So what's for dinner?"

Amber shrugged her shoulders. "I've got some steaks. Do you want me to grill them up?"

"Steaks? Is that all? Do you have vegetables, maybe some potatoes to go along with it? How about a desert?"

"Sure…" said Amber.

Michael shook his head in disbelief. "I mean, is that all you do now days? You just creep around the house in your tight-ass jeans with cutesy, little blouse and type away on your phone? What are you doing, if you don't mind me asking?"

Without warning, Amber suddenly exploded. "You know, Michael; what is your problem? It's like you've got some kind of problem with me just because the wheelchair lift is broken! That's all you do, now! You look for one reason after another to be mad at me!"

Michael stood up, sighed and walked towards the basement door. "I'm going downstairs."

And that's where Michael belonged in Amber's mind: deep, down in the cave to spend time with his deceased wife. In the meantime, Amber threw the steaks on the outside grill along with a few potatoes. Then she dumped a frozen bag of mixed vegetables in a plastic bowl and microwaved them. She didn't have to go out of her way to make Michael a special dinner. He was being an ass, and deserved harsh treatment. The man had it pretty good for all those years. Amber was beginning to feel taken for granted.

With Michael down in the cave, Amber found it the perfect opportunity to call Alex the Plumber and vent her frustrations. She stood outside near the grill and softly spoke to the very man who was responsible for all the trouble. "My husband is being such an ass. He's asking me what's for dinner, as-if he expects it. He totally takes me for granted. Then he was complaining about the way I dress, and even asked what I was doing on the phone. And he's mad at me for the wheelchair lift! I don't know why he thinks I'm responsible for the lift!"

Poor Amber; at least she had Alex to confide in!

An hour-and-a-half later, Michael emerged from the basement with half-drunk bottle of Pinot Noir and a full wine glass that was discarded in the sink. On the kitchen table sat a single place setting with an empty glass. There was a platter near the place setting with aluminum foil covering it. Next to it sat a covered, plastic bowl of mixed vegetables. Amber sat outside on the deck, watching Trista play on her jumbo playground. Apparently, Michael was to eat dinner alone, tonight.

But Michael had something important to ask his wife. She looked over to the screen door as it slid open and her husband walked out. To further demonstrate her anger towards Michael, she looked away and continued to watch Trista on the playground.

Michael was finally near. "Amber?"

"What?"

"I want to ask you something, and I want an honest answer."

Amber was cold in her reply, "Sure…"

"Do you have a man coming over here while I'm gone?"

This questioned outraged Amber. "Oh my gosh! Are you serious? I can't believe you, Michael! Are you accusing me of having an affair?"

"Well that's pretty much what having a man come over means."

At first, Amber's voice was low. "How dare you…" Then Amber screamed in a terrible fury, "*How dare* **you!** I run your house, take care of your invalid daughter, cook for you, try to make sex good for you; and you accuse me of having an affair? How dare you! You can sleep in your office, tonight! And you might as well get used to that being your bedroom for a while!"

Michael said nothing in return. He only walked back into the house and ate his dinner in solitude.

And rest assured, Amber confided in her secret friend of that humiliating moment as she whispered on the cell phone later that night. "He actually asked me if I was having an affair—wanted to know if I have someone come over while he's gone. Where would he get that crazy idea?" Then Amber paused, "Oh my gosh! I just realized; that little bitch told him. Paulette told my husband. She must have heard us on that night you broke the wheelchair lift. I'll take care of her the next time my husband goes out of town."

* * *

Next time wasn't too far into the future. On the following Wednesday, Michael announced a need to make a business trip on Friday morning. He wouldn't return until Sunday afternoon. Along with that, Michael made much improvement in his behavior at home. Receiving the silent treatment—Amber only communicating with her husband when necessary—along with Michael sleeping on the sofa in his office must have given him plenty of time to reconsider his inappropriate behavior.

The wheelchair lift had been repaired, and Paulette's presence returned to the lower level during the day. And of course, Amber continued to creep around the house while typing away at the cell phone. With Michael going out of town, big plans were underway for Amber and Alex on Saturday night. As for Friday; Alex, unfortunately, had some kind of date with his wife and couldn't get out of it. Such a disappointment! But at least they could spend Saturday night together.

And in addition to preparing for Saturday night, much planning was also underway of how to punish Paulette and discourage her from being Father's little spy.

Michael left Friday afternoon and everything appeared to Paulette to be normal. The wheelchair lift continued to function, and there were no voices of strange men in the house on Friday night. And much to Paulette's surprise, Amber entered the bedroom, bright and early on Saturday morning, making mention of giving Paulette her daily bath. In recent years, this was most unusual. Amber usually let Paulette's bath go for at least the first day of Father's absence.

This morning, Amber brought with her a tea cup. "Good morning! So how did you sleep last night?"

Suddenly, Paulette did not trust Amber.

"I started drinking green tea. It has plenty of antioxidants, but I can't seem to get it strong enough." Amber pulled the tea bag in and out of the cup to maximize its steeping effect. Then she placed it on Paulette's dresser. "Come on; let's get you in the bathroom to do your business."

Once Paulette completed her morning business on the toilet, she was next suspended in midair and undressed for her daily bath. Amber turned on the bath water, and adjusted the temperature. On this morning, the water needed to be nice and warm. Hotter... hotter... hotter... Amber continued to adjust the water until her finger instinctively pulled away out of discomfort. There, now the water was warm enough! Paulette had strawberry, red hair just like Linsey. Her skin was so delicate and pale, and probably very sensitive to extreme temperature.

Of course the water wasn't boiling hot! Amber certainly didn't have in mind to cause burns to Paulette. She only wished to shock her, maybe cause some uncomfortable scalding to Paulette's legs. While the tub filled with water, Amber went over to Paulette's dresser for her nice cup of green tea with bag that continued to steep.

Satisfied that the tub was full, Amber turned off the water. The heat and steam could be felt rising from the tub as Amber leaned over. Finally, Paulette was wheeled over, and the crane slowly lowered her paralyzed body into the bath water. While this happened, Amber took a couple sips of her tea.

In her condition, would Paulette be able to feel the pain? Perhaps she wouldn't realize the scalding until looking down at her legs. Oh, but Paulette definitely felt it as soon as the bottoms of her thighs and buttocks made contact with the water! Her head tilted back in the only reaction possible. Then Paulette began to scream out, signaling something terribly wrong. Amber was the only person who could help her in that moment. Surely she wouldn't let the paralyzed, young woman suffer.

But Amber only watched in amazement for a brief moment before setting her tea cup down. The damage to Paulette's spine must have been made in such a way that it only prevented movement, yet allowed her to have sensation.

Poor Paulette continued to frantically scream and thrash her head. Her long, straight, strawberry, red hair violently shook along her face, shoulders and neck. All alone on an early, Saturday morning with Father out of town; there was no one, outside of Amber, who could hear the screams. The bathroom door was locked shut; Paulette's bedroom door closed; and Trista's door had been shut that morning as well. The bathroom had been converted into an isolated torture chamber, many miles from civilization.

Amber showed extreme concern as she quickly approached the tub. "What? What is it, Honey?" She felt the bath water. "Oh no! I made the bath water too hot. I'm so sorry!" She immediately flipped the lever on the crane device to raise Paulette out of the water. Then she turned the bath water to cold and pulled the faucet open so it would balance the temperature to something more comfortable.

Paulette cried and whimpered like a little girl as she lay suspended in midair. But Amber didn't feel the least-bit sorry for her. Paulette was a woman, and she tried to play hardball with Amber. This morning was only a little sample of how Amber played back. Maybe next time Paulette would think twice before providing information to Father in secrecy.

Paulette's usually virgin, white skin was now lobster-red. "Oh, look at your legs! I scalded them! I'm so sorry." As cold water continued to fill the tub, Amber placed a wash rag under the faucet and then gently padded Paulette's thighs and legs to provide cooling comfort. "They'll be alright. At least it wasn't boiling water like my cup of tea. I bet you felt like tea bag being steeped in a cup!"

Then Amber looked down at the tub. "Oops! I bet I'm making the water too cold, now!" She bent down towards the faucet and re-adjusted the water so that it was warmer and would hopefully balance the tub to a desirable temperature. "There, we'll let that fill up some more and let you sit in some lukewarm water. Again, I'm so sorry."

Amber wasn't quite done with Paulette. This is why she let the water fill, nearly to the top of the tub. Amber needed to have a little talk with her adopted daughter, explain that it was best not to get over her head in causing trouble. "Uh-oh; I think maybe I filled the tub too high. That's okay, you should be fine."

The crane slowly lowered terribly-concerned Paulette back into the tub.

"Oh Honey, don't worry! I'm not going to let you go under the water and drown. How would I explain that to your father? I was in hot water throughout the week, remember? For some reason, your father was mad at me for the wheelchair lift. Imagine the trouble I would be in if you drowned."

Keep in mind that Paulette hadn't played in a swimming pool since before her bicycle accident. The sudden sensation of being weightless in a large tub of water, and unable to move, caused much panic for Paulette. How easy would it be for her bottom to suddenly lose grip and her head to go under?

Amber tilted Paulette's head back and gently poured water over her hair. "You're just so fortunate to have me here, taking care of you each day. You know I would never do anything to deliberately hurt you." Amber couldn't wait for the moment of lifting Paulette's legs out of the water to wash them. In doing so, it would be very possible to tug one of Paulette's legs, ever-so slightly, but enough to pull her under the water.

A few minutes passed as Paulette's face and arms were washed. "People always ask me why I don't have you sent to a nursing home. I'm like, 'No way! I feel like Paulette is my own daughter.' I could never do that."

Then, as Amber lifted Paulette's right leg out of the water, she did so in such a way that a tug was given, pulling the paralyzed women under, her head fully submerged. Amber was quick to rescue Paulette! She lifted her by the armpits and made contact with Paulette's soft breasts. With her head out of the water, Paulette choked while desperately gasping for air. Again, it had been many years since playing in water. She was unfamiliar with holding her breath.

Imagine the terror and panic! Finally able to breathe, Paulette cried some more like a frightened, little girl.

Amber was apologetic. "Oh my! That was scary! I'm so sorry! I'm just batting a hundred, today. I've scalded you and now I nearly drowned you. You're probably thinking, 'What did I do?' Again, I'm so sorry."

Through the years, Amber developed a certain intuition between her and Paulette. While dressing Paulette for the day, Amber noticed that her adopted daughter had a sudden surge of goose bumps, followed by tears that formed in her eyes. Apparently, she was deeply saddened and hurt by the morning's punishment. And then Paulette looked directly into Amber's eyes. Amber knew exactly what Paulette was saying.

"How could you do that to me? You know I wouldn't have told my father. I realize how dependent I am of you."

Amber believed Paulette was merely feeling sorry for herself in that moment. Paulette knew very well why she had been punished. There was no reason to deny what she had done.

Chapter Twenty-three

There is good reason for not seeking revenge or taking matters into your own hands. Although it may certainly feel good at the moment vengeance is finally delivered; some time later, the intense, negative emotions subside which allows reasoning to be restored. It is during this time that a person begins to regret the delivered punishment. "Was I seeing things clearly? Did I overreact?"

This is how Amber began to feel later that morning. While doing Saturday housework, an overall weekly cleaning, she continuously replayed the sad image of Paulette's teary eyes that asked, "How could you? You know I didn't tell my father."

Amber would quickly dispel these thoughts. "Yeah, right! Where else would Michael have gotten that idea? That snotty, little bitch can communicate without words to her father."

Again, the teary eyes would beckon from Amber's imagination. Amber knew things in her heart. She knew people for who they truly were. For this matter, Amber knew that Paulette said not a word of her suspicions or of the things heard on the night Alex disabled the lift.

Soon it became impossible to dispel the realization. Paulette truly was innocent, but had been senselessly tortured by having her legs scalded and then her head submerged under water.

What happened to Amber? Why was she seemingly possessed by a sudden, evil force?

Years ago, Amber sat at that very bathtub with tears in her own eyes, asking Paulette to give her a chance, suggesting that the two could become friends. And Paulette did become a friend of Amber's. Of course due to the unusual circumstances, there was often some rocky ground. But the two laughed and cried together. Paulette listened attentively to Amber's own life stories. In a way, she allowed Amber to become her new mother, all for the sake of sanctifying the love between Amber and Father.

And how did Amber thank Paulette? In recent years, she let her go unbathed for a few days with greasy hair, scummy teeth and in the same sleepwear so that Paulette could smell her own stench. And if that wasn't bad enough, Amber was seeking clever ways to keep Paulette confined in solitude to her own room. This morning's treatment was by far the worse. How Amber began to hate herself more and more as the morning passed.

Some time after lunch, under further guilt, Amber began to speculate a new theory of Michael's awareness. His question of Amber having a man in the house while away came shortly after his visit to Linsey's chamber. Of course! It was the blasted statue-head that tormented Amber for eight, long years. Although nothing more than a morbid piece of art, the relic gave Michael the power of clairvoyance; most likely brought on by the guided spirit of Linsey.

Linsey was the cause of discord in the home, she did it all. How ungrateful the deceased woman was. Amber rescued Michael and Paulette in one of their darkest hours. She adopted Paulette and cared for her in the best way that a stranger could. And in witnessing the ugly, physical and mental changes in Michael that were brought on by old age; Amber did something far, less damaging than leave her husband. She merely found a male companion to substitute the lack of closeness and affection that she so desperately needed. Did Linsey really think she could have done any better? How would she have reacted if still alive and married to the horrible beast that Michael had become? What an ungrateful, troublesome bitch Linsey was!

The time had come to end Linsey's reign of terror. That thing underground was so unhealthy for Michael, anyway. But Amber wouldn't waste her time in only wishing for Linsey to go away; hope for a strong gust of wind to blow through a chimney in the cave and knock the statue-head over. Amber desired the long-fully yearned pleasure of killing Linsey with her own two hands. Aside from that, doing the job any other way would only prove how fearful she was of the relic. The time had come for Amber to venture alone into the dimly-lit chamber, and face Linsey with all her resentment.

Always bring a flashlight when venturing into the cavern. That was the most important rule given to Amber on that morning of December 24th, some eight years ago. After flipping on the industrial-sized light switch, Amber was certain to reach for the flashlight and test it before trekking down the fifty foot, de-clining hallway that was illuminated by industrial track lighting.

While following the illuminated path in the cavern, Amber was sure to take note of the recognizable and most prominent rock formations to use as a guide for returning. "Yes Linsey, Michael taught me well. He showed me, *exactly*, how to get to your chamber. I still remember." Amber continued to follow the illuminated path downward while speaking out loud to Lin-sey. "You just couldn't enjoy your own chamber where Michael would come visit you. You had to interfere with our marriage."

Past two chambers and three more to go, the depth and spiral-ing darkness of the cavern began to play with Amber's imagina-tion. Often she would pass some small rock formation or grotto that would remind her of the silhouette of the statue-head. This would further remind her of the nightmare of the statue-head growling and flashing its teeth. At some point, the memory was nearly hallucinogenic as she could see with such clarity a vision of that frightening dream. The sound of remembered growling echoed in Amber's head. The sensation of terror returned, exactly as felt on a winter's night some eight years ago. Was it a warning to go away? Was Linsey speaking to Amber through visions? Perhaps this was the clairvoyant effect that Michael experienced.

But Amber was stronger than that! She called out, "I'm coming for you, Linsey! You dead, rotten bitch; I'm coming for you! You've screwed with my life long enough!" Her voice echoed throughout the cavern, then drowned under the sound of echoing water.

Deeper and deeper Amber hiked as her anxiety grew. Surely the statue-head would be alive as in the dream. It would take sight of Amber entering the chamber and begin to growl. Perhaps it would speak criticism in its final moments. "You pathetic excuse of a woman: you consider yourself to be a mother and wife? You're nothing more than a selfish, little tramp that neglects her children and deceives her husband."

These words would only be lies. Amber knew she was so, much more; only going through a difficult moment in her life. The hurtful words would be such bold statements, made by a helpless head that could do nothing but watch as a smash to its face is given.

Ah, but what if Linsey wasn't inanimate? What if through the years she had gained more power? What if through the spirit of Linsey's intervention, the head could roll off the grotto and along the floor to chase Amber? Her sharp teeth could bite at Amber's legs and tear away flesh. It would be such a terrifying moment, causing Amber to run out of the chamber. Linsey might even be able to roll all the way up the cavern and back into the wine cellar with Amber only a few feet away. Hopefully Amber could close and lock the door before the thing made its way through. But then it would continuously roll against the door as-if knocking. Michael would discover Linsey there. And in all the power of that relic, it would give account to Amber's attempted murder.

Amber stopped just past the fourth chamber. She didn't have much traveling left to go, but there was still time to turn around and avoid a terrifying encounter with Linsey. The thing truly was powerful. The deeper Amber traveled, the more she realized how much life the relic possessed. It created irrational fears, and provided negative insights into Amber's own life. The statue-head of Linsey was nothing short of evil.

But Amber pressed onward. "I'm coming, Linsey! Your final moments are near!" She picked up her pace to a light jog in an effort to tolerate the heart-pounding adrenaline. This was not going to be an easy fight.

Finally, Amber noticed the soft glow through an arched entryway. Michael must have lit jumbo, devotional candles in the chamber. "I'm here, Linsey! I'm here!" She walked through the entryway and took sight of the statue-head. Linsey sat on the medium-sized grotto that was surrounded by several candle fixtures. Through the dim, flickering light, she looked as alive as ever and wearing a scornful expression.

Amber merely extended her fornications to Linsey. She wouldn't allow Linsey to get the best of her. She approached the grotto, and noticed that Michael had set several picture frames near the statue-head. They were pictures of her and Michael in younger years; pictures of a family vacation—probably the last one before Linsey became ill—and a picture of when Linsey was very young, probably around the time when she and Michael started dating. Linsey definitely resembled the young Amber at that age.

Amber looked up at the statue-head. Now it wore a peaceful expression, relieved to have finally had her talk with Amber. "That's all it is, Honey... that's all he wants... it's not easy, I know; but you can be so much better... do you understand, now?"

Of course Linsey would change her story, try to put Amber at ease. The evil relic could wear any expression, and the kindness at that moment was its best defense. As far as Amber was concerned, that thing had caused more than enough grief in her life. It would continue to torment Amber had she turned from the chamber and walked back to the wine cellar. To prevent this, Amber grasped Linsey by the back of her long, strawberry-red hair; raised the statue-head so that her face suspended high above Amber's and then threw her down—face first—onto the floor of the chamber. The statue-head broke into three pieces.

But Amber wasn't done, yet! Only broken into three pieces wasn't nearly enough damage to compensate the years of grief Linsey caused. Amber pulled a candle fixture from the ground and repeatedly smashed it against Linsey's head until she was broken into a dozen small pieces. Amber would have liked to have ignited Linsey's hair with the candle flame at first impact. But the movement caused the flame to die out. That was okay; there were other candles lit in the chamber. She reached for one and slowly brought it close to Linsey's long, strawberry-red, beautiful hair. But the blasted wig was fire retardant! Amber resorted to angrily smashing open the picture frames on the grotto and then burning each photo, one-by-one. There could be no remnant of Linsey in that chamber by the time the job was done.

As the last picture burned, Amber stepped back to examine the horrible murder. Satisfied, she turned from the chamber and head back for the wine cellar.

* * *

Tonight was a special night. Only one week from Independence Day weekend, Amber and Alex decided to celebrate the holiday, as being together would most likely be impossible the following weekend. By 9:30, both Trista and Paulette were in bed for the night. Outside, Amber had a roast-leg-of-lamb rotating on the grill. In the refrigerator, vegetable shish-kabobs marinated in a container. When the roast was nearly done, Amber would put the kabobs on the grill. Amber even went so far as to make a tiramisu for desert. Alex was a great guy, and he deserved a wonderful meal!

It was no longer necessary to reach for Alex's business card for a late night call. Amber had his number preprogrammed in her own cell phone as she texted him throughout the day. At 9:45, she gave his number a call. "I need you to come over and check out my plumbing." Of course this was said seductively!

A half-hour later, the plumbing van pulled into the over-sized horseshoe driveway of the Dickly castle. Tonight, Alex was dressed sharp; clean and shaven, and carrying a small bouquet of roses. Alex was such a sweet guy!

Living in the Dickly castle brought with it the luxury of a fully-stocked bar in the basement. Any Fourth of July party starts off with some drinks. After passionately kissing Alex in the foyer, Amber invited him to the bar in the basement. "Let's start you off with a drink."

Halfway through their first round of long island iced teas, Amber suddenly had the crazy idea of showing Alex the secret cavern of the Dickly castle. "I want to show you something; follow me."

The two entered the wine cellar, and Alex was immediately impressed. "Whoa! You people drink a lot of wine!"

"It's mostly my husband's. We used to open a bottle every night, but that hasn't happened in quite some time."

"Do you mind?" Alex motioned towards the wine rack, indicating his desire to crack open a bottle.

"No, go ahead! There's a couple thousand bottles in here. Michael will never notice."

Alex looked around and pulled a bottle. "Pinot Noir…" Outside of Merlot, Alex didn't know the first thing about wine. Pinot

Noir sounded sophisticated and high class. Little did he know that it was Linsey's private reserve. On one of the tables of the wine cellar sat a cork screw that was usually used to open a bottle of Pinot Noir whenever Michael visited Linsey. Now, just hours after Linsey's murder, Alex used it to open and take a swig from one of Linsey's bottles.

Feeling Alex was satisfied with his bottle of wine, Amber announced, "This isn't what I wanted to show you."

Alex was surprised, "No? You have something else?"

Amber opened the small door that led to the declining hallway, flipped on the industrial light switch and grabbed the flashlight. "Follow me."

Alex paused at the entryway of the cavern. "Whoa! What's down there? You got some kind of kinky torture chamber?"

Amber smiled, "You'll see." She continued to descend the hallway.

When finally at the bottom, both turned left. It took a few seconds for Alex to realize what he was seeing. "You've got a cave!"

At that very moment, a taxi cab pulled into the entrance of inclined driveway of the Dickly castle and made it's ascent up the miniature mountain. Michael sat in the backseat, dressed in casual clothes with a grave expression on his face. He announced to the driver, "Listen, I want you to do me a really, big favor."

"Sure, what's that?"

"When we get close to the house, can you turn your headlights off? My driveway has lights, so you can still see."

In his years of driving, the cabbie had seen plenty of interesting behavior from people. This same scenario had been played out at least once every few months. He knew Michael's story all, too well. A traveling businessman suspected his wife of being unfaithful. He staged another out-of-town trip, and was coming home early to surprise his wife. The cabbie winked to Michael in the rearview mirror, "Gocha… let me know when you want me to turn out the lights."

"Sure; and if you can drop me off before reaching the horseshoe driveway, that would be great."

It wasn't necessary for the customer to explain further. He wished not to alarm his unfaithful wife at the sound of a cab door closing. "Absolutely… whatever you need. And I hope everything works out for you."

Soon, the taxi cab reached the top of Dickly Mountain. Michael called out, "Okay, can you kill the lights? Let me out here."

"Sure!" The cabbie parked and took payment from Michael. "Best of luck to you, Sir. You want me to wait here, just in case?"

"No, that won't be necessary."

Michael exited the cab, and immediately took notice of the plumbing van parked near the house. "Plumber, huh?" He walked up to the well-lit, grand entrance; hoping no one had taken sight from inside. Then he slowly opened the front door and stepped into the grand foyer.

Outside of the kitchen, much of the lighting in the house was off. Surely Amber was in bed with the plumber. That's where every other scenario of a similar nature ends. It made perfect sense for Michael to tiptoe up the stairs.

But no one was in Michael's bed with his wife. No one sat, naked, in the master bath hot-tub with champagne. Michael further investigated the other rooms on the second level. Where were Amber and the supposed plumber?

Back on the main level, he heard the faint sound of the motorized spit, rotating on the grill. Was Amber outside with her boyfriend? Michael carefully opened the back screen door and smelled the delicious aroma of a roast nearly done. Out of curiosity, he approached the grill and took sight of the tempting, juicy, roast-leg-of-lamb that slowly rotated above the flames. There was definitely a late night party happening at the Dickly castle, and Michael was not invited. To combat his hurt feelings, he reached for a small knife that rested at the edge of the bar-beque, turned off the motorized spit and then helped himself to a slice of lamb. Of course it was necessary to blow on the meat while carefully taking a bite. But it was roast-leg-of-lamb, grilled outside, and something Michael wasn't invited to enjoy. How good it felt to crash their little party. Now if Michael could only find them, the party-crashing would be all the better.

Was Amber in the basement with the plumber? Perhaps they went downstairs to mix up some drinks. Chewing the remains of the slice of meat, Michael went back into the house and towards the basement. Sure enough, it appeared well-lit while approach-ing the stairwell. Amber was probably naked and bent over the bar while the plumber bounced off her behind. It was best to slowly and softly descend the stairs and then clear his throat at a moment when the two could finally see him.

But outside of two partially finished drinks, no one was at the bar. No one sat or lay on the sofa or chairs in the well-furnished basement. Michael did notice, however, the door to his wine cellar was open. He thought for a moment that perhaps he should hide and only come out when the party livened up. But it was awfully quiet in the wine cellar. Maybe Amber and her boyfriend were making out in there—possibly more.

No one was in the wine cellar, but Michael immediately no-ticed that the small door to the cavern was wide open. In addi-tion, the flashlight that normally hung on the wall was missing. Not only did Amber have a man in the house, but she invited this stranger into Michael's sacred, private world. Michael jour-neyed further, down the declining hallway, in search of his un-faithful wife.

He speculated that perhaps his timing was poor. What if Michael only discovered Amber and the plumber, hiking along the illuminated trail of the cavern?

Upon discovery and in a jealous rage, Michael would ask, "What are you doing down here, Amber?"

"What? I'm just showing my friend the cavern. I thought he would like it."

"Why do you have a man in the house while I'm gone?"

"He's a friend, Michael; just a friend! You don't have to draw any conclusions."

When taken at face value, Amber wouldn't be doing anything wrong. She could argue this for many hours. There is no crime for having a friend who just so happens to be a man. If Michael persisted, he might look like a jealous and possessive husband. Was he doing the right thing by surprising Amber in the cavern?

Ah, but Michael certainly did the right thing! Much to his surprise, Amber was naked and bent over a large boulder that was off the side of the trail. With his pants down to his ankles, the plumber stood behind Amber, thrusting and slamming against Amber's behind. Apparently, desert was being had before dinner.

If seeing Amber scream out in pleasure wasn't hurtful enough, Michael also took notice of the bottle of wine that the plumber occasionally took a swig from. Even from a distance, Michael could see the words, Pinot Noir. Not only was the plumber banging Michael's wife, but he found a way to defile precious Linsey as well.

In such a numb state, Michael could only observe in silence. But then the plumber soon noticed there was company.

"Crap!" yelled Alex.

"What? What's wrong?"

"Your husband, I think."

Amber looked over and sure enough, Michael stood motionless with a sad expression.

And how would you expect Amber to react? She said what any other cheating spouse says when discovered with a lover. "Michael, it's not what you think!"

If ever caught in bed with someone other than your spouse, don't bother with such an insulting statement. It only provokes anger in the person who is hurt. For Michael, it pulled him out of the sad, numb state as he growled in a terrible fury, "Not what I think? I come home and find some strange man, bouncing off my wife's naked ass! What the hell do you expect me to think?"

But Amber persisted, "I'm sorry Michael! Please believe me!"

As for Alex, he moved further and further away from Amber while desperately pulling up his boxers and pants. Excusing himself was not necessary. Amber's furious husband discovered another man screwing her. And although Amber's husband was an old man, there was the possibility that he had a gun. Aside from that, the company van was in the driveway with telephone number printed in large, bold letters. If Alex was lucky, the furious husband wouldn't have copied the information before entering the house. And wouldn't you know it: the solid hunk-of-a-man looked at the ground in shame, nearly cowered from Michael while passing by.

It was the last time Amber would see Alex. But she wouldn't run after him. Most important at that moment was her furious husband, who needed reassurance that what was seen wasn't meant. Naked, she carefully approached Michael, "I'm sorry, Michael. I'm so sorry! It's not what you think!"

Michael growled in return, "I don't want to hear it right now!"

Frightened, Amber ran past her husband and up the inclined hallway that led back to the wine cellar. Yes, she was naked; still in shock from being discovered by Michael. By the time she reached the bedroom and put on some clothes, serious guilt and regret filled her. She sat at the edge of the bed, and waited for Michael. She would take anything from him—shouting, insults, shoves to the wall or slaps to the face. Amber deserved it all! She had been such a bitch in recent weeks.

But Amber might as well have packed her bags. Sabotaging the wheelchair lift; scalding and nearly drowning Paulette;

inviting a strange man in the house for sex while Michael was gone: these things didn't come close to the horrible thing that Michael was about to discover.

Alone in the cavern, Michael suddenly longed for Linsey. Linsey would have never done this to him. How Michael needed comfort from the woman who truly loved him. Time alone with her might have provided the strength and insight to handle the recent crisis.

Michael slowly and sadly descended the trail, passing every chamber and taking notice of the landmarks along the way. Linsey was with him now. Her words could nearly be heard in his heart, "It's terrible, I know. But she's only going through a difficult time. Remember when I was in my early thirties and got a little, too close to the butcher? We got through it, remember? This is worse than what I did, but you are older and wiser now."

Perhaps Linsey was right. Amber married in her early twenties which might have made the seven-year-itch all the more difficult. Aside from that, Michael had been distant in the past couple of years, not to mention boring. Every conversation centered on money, business or investments. Idle conversation? Unless there was something constructive or had some practical agenda, there was no need to talk. Of course Amber would have resolved to outside companionship.

How fortunate Michael was to have Linsey watch over him. But what was this? As he entered her chamber, Linsey's face did not sit on the grotto and greet him. Instead, two of the devotional candles lay on the floor, almost pointing to the tragic aftermath of a messy murder. Linsey's long, beautiful, strawberry-red hair lay stretched and mangled on the ground. Only a portion of her forehead and scalp remain attached. Surrounding the reminder of what used to be Linsey were some dozen pieces of her beautiful face. Michael picked up a piece that would have been Linsey's right cheek, followed by only a portion of her upper lip. When alive, these two pieces were only a fragment of what would have helped create a smile, and possibly led to laughter.

Michael sorted through the mess, desperately searching for something that would have been Linsey's nose. The next recognizable piece was a corner of her right eyebrow and temple. And where were Linsey's eyes? In life, both eyes were the softest and most brilliant blue that could melt anyone from a distance. Perhaps seeing this could have made Michael feel better. At least he still had his favorite photos of her. But much to his horror, the pictures of Linsey that sat on the grotto were missing. All that remained were smashed picture frames. He assumed that the snapshots of Linsey's happy moments had been burned.

All Michael could do was lie on the floor, eyes closed with his head buried in Linsey's hair. How long would it be before memory failed him, and Linsey's face could no longer be recalled? He had other photos upstairs, but none stirred his heart like the ones that had been destroyed.

Loss of job, crashed business, terrible illness and injury, death of a close family member, or—even worse—death of a wife: there is a moment in a man's life, a turning point that alters him forever and usually serves as a precursor to old age. Whatever your poison, I hope that life makes it as painless and least-destructive. As for Michael, he lost the woman he loved so dearly not once, but twice.

Lightning Source UK Ltd.
Milton Keynes UK
UKHW022013030521
383075UK00010B/792/J